Return to
Eslinar

Return to
Eslinar

A. C. WHEELER

iUniverse

RETURN TO ESLINAR

iUniverse books may be ordered through booksellers or by contacting:

iUniverse
1663 Liberty Drive
Bloomington, IN 47403
www.iuniverse.com
844-349-9409

ISBN: 978-1-4917-7500-4 (sc)
ISBN: 978-1-4917-7501-1 (e)

Library of Congress Control Number: 2015915218

Print information available on the last page.

iUniverse rev. date: 02/28/2022

⮂ Chapter 1

THE OCEAN BREEZE STROKED SARAH'S HAIR AS SHE SIPPED her ritualistic morning brew on the balcony of the hotel room. She was able to enjoy the sweet aroma for the first time in as long as she could remember.

If she'd known what her decision to leave was going to do to her life, perhaps she would have changed her mind and stayed, but like so many other things, it is only at the end that we see what our decisions have meant.

A composed peace came over Sarah as she looked out over the sea. To her, the ocean side was a sanctuary, a place to rest despite the world bustling about on the street below.

Holding her mug close, Sarah looked out past the streets and buildings and let the beautiful early-morning sky embrace her spirit. The sun was trying to peek around the few clouds that still lingered from the storm the night before. Sarah wondered how there was still room enough for such a small woman. The idea had baffled her since she was a child, and when her mind was at rest, she still pondered the facts of her own existence.

When the coffee was finished, Sarah came out of her quiet moment of contemplation and decided to get ready to leave on her adventure. The idea of roaming across the country—untethered to job, home, or responsibility—had always captured Sarah's imagination, which made her decision to try it that much more exciting to her.

Knowing she wouldn't have any particular place to stay, she had spent considerable time packing her backpack with the proper provisions. All looked good; she was as packed and as ready as she would ever be.

As the water warmed for a shower, Sarah looked in the mirror that hung directly over the sink. She hadn't slowed down enough in some time to take notice of the beautiful young woman she had blossomed into despite the signs of stress from the high-paced, never-ending pressure of her job.

The shower was intentionally long, and the water was perfect to her liking. By the time Sarah got out, dried off, and wrapped the supplied terry-cloth robe around her, she was more than ready for the four-course breakfast that was delivered by room service. She set herself up at the small table and enjoyed what she feared would be her last full meal for a while.

After tying her hair back into a ponytail, Sarah put on long denim shorts and a long-sleeved green T-shirt. It was warm out, but the weather station was calling for a cool breeze later on. She didn't want to be concerned with changing. All packed, bathed, fed, and dressed, Sarah was ready. It was nearly noon when she checked out, making sure to compliment the service as she left.

Taking a deep breath of clean ocean air, Sarah started toward the boardwalk. She couldn't help but notice the sky had turned a beautiful shade of aqua, which, as nice as it was to look at, meant rain. Despite that knowledge, she kept her head up and enjoyed the serenity that just being there gave her.

As she walked, Sarah's mind started to wander to what her coworkers would do without her. She had spent so much time and energy making herself needed there that she was having a hard time letting go. Who would run out to the latest happenings to get the pictures needed for the paper's morning printing? Who would travel to the places no one else wanted to go to capture real life on film? Her job had become her whole life; it was very close to being the sole definition of her identity. Taking herself out of it was a difficult choice. She had friends and mentors there, and she was close to the promotion she had been working for. Her mental obsession with it was enough to confirm that the vacation was the right medicine for her. Many people questioned her timing, but it was something she just needed to do.

Sarah had made a point to visit her mother before checking into the hotel the night before. Grattiella was not exactly happy about Sarah's decision to "roam about," but, in character, she supported her choice. She'd reminded Sarah of the dangers in the world, as if Sarah didn't know, and sent her off with a little extra cash, an extra bundle of food, and lots of extra hugs.

Sarah's journey started out calmly, and she wondered what her mother had been making such a fuss about. As she walked, she glanced over at the hustling boardwalkers a few times, but she mostly daydreamed about her life as she watched the waves come in and out.

After a long while walking and thinking, Sarah started

to get hungry. The top of a nearby sand dune looked like a good place to sit and eat. To her relief, she found another spot that was tucked farther away and quickly went to it. Relieving herself outdoors was not something Sarah was used to, but she made do since she had to.

After taking a few bites of her rationed food, she realized how dark it had become. Finding a suitable shelter became priority. With that thought, as if following a script, a low rumble came from the southern skies. The sky became a deep gray, and the clouds were moving fast. She knew she needed to find shelter quickly.

Off in the distance, she saw a patch of trees that marked the end of her stretch of beach. Sarah grabbed her backpack and began to run as fast as she could in a futile attempt to get to the trees before the rain got to her. When she breached the front line of the brush, her hair was drenched, and her shirt hung low with rainwater. She looked out from the shelter of the green canopy, and the size and amount of rain that fell impressed her.

With a rush of confidence, Sarah walked into the forest to find a place to set up camp for the night. The forest was like nothing she had seen before. It was dark in places, and sporadic beams of light broke through despite the storm. Although she could still hear the ocean, she could, to her surprise, no longer see it.

After a brief walk, she found herself near an old, sturdy tree. Sarah put down her backpack, took out some of her gear, and started out for firewood. The goal was to get back to the campsite before the sparse illumination faded to black.

Finding wood dry enough to burn was no easy task.

After a while, she managed to get an armful, and back at her makeshift camp, she made a fire that would have impressed any scout. It burned just enough to create warmth for her and her food. It gave off protective light, but it did not rise high enough to endanger even the lowest branches.

After finishing her rationed meal, she took a journal and pencil from her bag. Lying near the fire, she began to write.

> It is the first night of my journey, and thus far, other than a bit of rain, it has been quite uneventful. I will admit to you that I don't know why I am doing this. I can only say for sure that after being alone with my own thoughts and with nature for this one day, I really needed the rest. Maybe I will find something more to tell you about tomorrow.

Putting the pencil and journal away, Sarah used her pack as a pillow. She watched the fire until sleep took over and dreams flooded her mind.

After a short while, Sarah was jolted awake. She sat up with her eyes as wide as possible. Whatever awoke her was a mystery, but it had come close enough to move the air by her head. A loud crack came from the tree above her. She stood up in a start, looking intently at the branches directly above her. It was almost morning, and the sun shone through the trees in such a way that shadows landed consistently on each limb, making it harder to find specific shapes. From behind, she heard another snap and spun to see. Sarah quickly became angry instead of frightened. She didn't like being toyed with. At the ready with her hunting knife, memories of her mother's warnings flooded her mind.

Sarah moved toward the spot where she'd heard the sound, but before she got there, she heard a giggle coming from where she had just been standing. Spinning about again, she saw a creature that was only half her size. It had crinkled skin and pointed ears.

She froze with astonishment when the creature said in a soft, crackling voice, "Too far you wander, miss."

"Who are you?" Sarah demanded.

"Aye, there will be time for intros another while. We are not safe here. Must go straightaway." The stranger motioned for Sarah to calm down.

"Not safe?" Sarah began to see the creature without the veil of fear and anger, and her breathing began to steady.

He was what some would call lean, but Sarah thought he looked rather skinny, which has a whole different meaning to most. He wore faded brown leather overalls, and he trotted over to her bag and threw it over his shoulder. "Let us be on our way, miss. 'Tis not safe." He motioned to her to follow.

Sarah was so stunned by the little man in front of her that she followed without another word. As they walked, she occasionally heard rustling sounds. She would have bet her career that she heard talking from the tips of the trees. With every step, the little man became quicker and more agile.

When they finally came to a clearing, the little man put down her bag and turned to her. "You were lucky, miss." He went over to her and began checking her out, much like a doctor would if he were looking for a parasite of some kind.

"What are you looking for? And why was I so lucky? And who are you? And where am I?" Sarah was getting exasperated.

Realizing the man had stopped, she looked down at him. His eyes became wide and strangely aware—of what, she could not say—but then he took a few steps back and pierced her eyes with his gaze. "Only one is which you could be if I's rememba me stories right." He scratched his head. "You have the look, and the poison didn't take. You be either luckier than an old Grink in a swamp full of mud, or you be the one I say. We will rest here. Then morning come, and I'll take you to Rika. He would full know."

Before his search for firewood, the strange little creature dug a fire pit. Sarah watched in amazement. She was still unconvinced that he was not merely a part of a very intense dream—the type of dream she had been known to have. Had it not been for the fresh pine scent, the cool breeze, and the warmth of the setting sun verifying authenticity for her, she wouldn't have thought it even remotely possible.

Her guide seemed to be very interested in her comfort. He set up her things for her, covered her with a small blanket, took out a pot from his own satchel, and began stirring up something to eat over the little fire he had made.

After what seemed like a very long while, the little man broke the silence. He said, "Tinbe is the name. I belong with the Gropal of the East." He looked up at her with the eyes of a very old soul. "It has been long since one like you has come to be here."

"Where is here?" Sarah asked.

Tinbe passed Sarah a wooden bowl of stew and sat with his own bowl. After a long, hearty gulp, he said, "You, lass, have many questions—sure of it I am. Here is Hofflinar. Not where we should be." He stood up, reached over the fire, and tapped her on the shoulder as if to reassure her. "But not bad as they come, though. Sleep now. Morning soon here, and gone we will go."

Tinbe rested on a bundle made from his satchel and motioned Sarah to also settle in for some rest. He had piled some leaves together and thrown a blanket down over them. Feeling like she didn't have too many options at that point since she was very tired from their day of walking, she lay down. The warmth from the fire soon engulfed her mind and body. Despite her efforts, slumber came to her, and the world around her fell quiet.

Tinbe sat up slowly with the rising sun. Stretching his upper half first and then standing to stretch the lower, he did his best to shake off the punishing effects of sleeping on the ground. Quietly moving over to Sarah, he said, "Miss?" Then Tinbe said in a louder tone, "Miss?" Sarah began to stir. "Miss, to go we must. Waking now would be good."

Sarah opened her eyes and sat straight up with startling speed.

Tinbe jumped back a good foot or so, a little shaken.

"I'm still here?" Sarah said in amazement.

"Wishing somewhere else to be?" Tinbe asked with puzzlement in his eyes. Shaking his head, Tinbe turned and began to pack up his satchel. He motioned to Sarah to do the same.

Still groggy, Sarah said, "I thought maybe this was a

dream, but I am awake—and here I am, and there you are."
She really didn't understand what had happened to her, and
something on her face must have spoken of her fear because
Tinbe went and sat by her.

"Be your name what?" he said in a soft, friendly tone.

She focused her beautiful blue eyes on him. "My name
is Sarah, and you are Tinbe, yes?"

"Ah, yes. Remembering you are." A small smile
appeared on Tinbe's worried face. "Worry you not. Dream
this is not, but safe you are for now. To keep safe, go we
must to Rika's lands. He will answer there."

Tinbe tapped her knee and grabbed her hand to help
her stand.

She made the decision at that moment to trust Tinbe,
which was a big deal for Sarah. Trusting didn't come easily
to her. She was confused, but she knew he meant her no
harm.

They started walking with Tinbe in the lead. Sarah was
keeping pace easily enough, but her mind was upside down
with the assurance from her guide that she was in fact not
dreaming as she had hoped.

"To the river, go we must," Tinbe shouted over his
shoulder. "Quick here you must be. Safety certain not about
us yet." He stopped a moment for both to catch their breath.

"You have said we're not safe before. Not safe from
what?" Sarah was feeling quite annoyed with the whole
situation. "I'm not going another step until you tell me
something, Mr. Tinbe."

Tinbe appeared shocked by Sarah's sudden outburst.
"Excuse rushing, Miss Sarah. Tell more must I." With fear
in his eyes, he walked straight up to Sarah. "Say this can I.

Behind us is my fear." Pointing to his right and to his left, he added, "There and there, enemies be. On this place, speak of no."

Sarah was no less annoyed, but she could feel in her heart that the fear in Tinbe's eyes was real. She pointed ahead for him to go.

After hiking for a while, if the jogging could be considered hiking, Sarah started to really look at her surroundings. They had made their way to a vast meadow teeming with unfamiliar plant life. She noticed that the bristles of the blades of grass swiped her legs as they went by, and every now and again, one would scratch her. Some of the cuts were not so bad, but some of them were deep and stung quite a lot. She stopped inwardly complaining about them when they got to the top of an incline. She gazed past Tinbe out to the horizon. The meadow was vast, and in the direction he kept pointing, they had a long way to go before she could tend to her wounds.

The sky was just as it had been on the beach. It was a tranquil blue with billowing clouds from east to west. Off in the distance, another forest stretched far to one end and farther still to the other end of the horizon.

By noon, they had almost reached the forest.

Tinbe motioned for her to stop. "Sarah, wait here."

He was about to dart off when Sarah called to him. "Just wait here?" She looked around and motioned her confusion to him.

He came back to her, and with a gentle hand on her arm, he said, "Not go far will I. Our arrival must I announce."

She watched him run off.

୫ Chapter 2

TRYING HARD TO DISTRACT HERSELF FROM THE VULNERABILITY she felt standing alone in the meadow, Sarah reached into the outer pouch of her sack and pulled out a snack bar. At home, she rarely ate that type of thing, but portable food had been her main concern when she packed her bag.

As she snacked on the bar and sipped from her canteen, Sarah looked around at the breathtaking contrast of the brilliant blue sky against the light tan meadow. Although she thought about how nice it would be to preserve the image on film, she knew that her choice to bring her journal instead was a good one. It would take longer to describe things she saw and experienced, but the change was a welcomed one.

She had started thinking about her mother when she saw the brush about fifty yards in front of her start to move. Out came Tinbe. He was accompanied by at least a dozen other creatures that were of his same height and build, but they all were different from him and each other. Her heart started to pound. She thought for a moment that she was certainly outnumbered, and she wondered if trusting Tinbe had been a mistake.

Most of Tinbe's companions stayed at the edge of the forest while Tinbe and two others approached Sarah. Tinbe had a great smile on his face and touched Sarah's arm as gently as before. "Excitement for you arriving is great. Come and be welcomed."

Sarah said, "What about Rika? You said we were going to go to Rika and that he would explain."

"Yes, Rika will." Tinbe put his small hand on her back and led her toward the forest. The other two escorts stayed a few paces behind.

When they reached the shadowy cover of the woods, Tinbe stopped and pointed to the others. "My brother 'tis he." A little man in a blue cloak bowed low. Then Tinbe pointed to his other side, "'Tis be me son." The even littler boy bowed like his uncle had.

The young lad grabbed Sarah's hand, and together they walked. All the while, he looked at Sarah and smiled as big a smile as she had ever seen. The pathway began to widen, and they emerged into a small city.

There were a few scattered huts on ground level, but for the most part, the city was built in the trees. As they walked, Sarah observed three youngsters piling lumber in a massive pit for the nightly fire. One table near the pit was covered with fruits and vegetables, and another was blanketed with pastries of every kind.

As far as her eyes could see, wooden huts littered the trees at all levels. Some were multilevel and designed well, and others looked like the tree house she knew as a child. The bridges that connected the structures were handsomely crafted. They were not just planks of wood tied together with rope to serve the purpose of crossing; they were amazing works of engineering and art, and designs were carved on every surface. The railings were made from glistening silver that melted in with the rope itself.

The people who came to welcome her began to disband, and Tinbe had her by the arm. "To your rest spot take you I will, food to come shortly."

He led her up one of the beautiful staircases into a hut that seemed a bit larger than most. She looked at the doorway and then at Tinbe, noting the size difference between them. It was certainly larger than he would have needed.

Tinbe smiled and said, "Right size, I thought?" With a smirk and a shrug, he ushered her inside. "Come get you we will for food, yes?"

Sarah looked at him with a cordial smile, but she was unable to hide her discomfort with the situation.

Tinbe sat her down on a small chair by the window. "Rest you must. Explaining is plenty, and plenty we will do. Guests we have tonight. Heard of you coming they did. You must be rested to hear with openness."

Although still confused, she no longer looked frightened. Tinbe gave Sarah a satisfied smile and left, closing the solid, beautifully carved wooden door behind him.

Sarah sat quietly for a few minutes, and then, for the first time in a long stretch, she noticed she had to go to the bathroom. Her body had had little time to be concerned with that function since meeting Tinbe. So the sight of a small facility adjacent to where she sat was most pleasing.

After addressing her bodily needs, Sarah took a good look around at the bathroom. The detailed carving was impressive even around the rim of the toilet. The large mirror that hung above the tiny sink was elegantly encased in a frame of carved wood and decorated with the silvery rope on its outer edges. At first, she was so interested in the carvings that she didn't pay attention to her own reflection.

Sarah's eyes finally wandered to the unsightly reflection in the mirror. Her hair was matted, and her skin was itchy, a result of an unharmonious combination of sweat and whatever earth she had slept on the night before.

Retrieving a rag from her bag, Sarah began to wipe her face, neck, and arms. Piling her tattered clothes in the corner, she worked methodically down her torso. As the water began to drip onto her legs, the slight sting from the many horizontal cuts along her calves began to worsen. As the painful wounds were cleaned, she realized she was not dreaming. In her many intense dreams, Sarah had never actually felt pain—no matter how violent the dreams were. Taking the ointment from her bag, she lifted her head, bit her lip, and applied it to one wound after another.

Having only packed one outfit, Sarah figured then was as good a time as any to change into it. The blue jeans slid easily over her thighs, and the white T-shirt fit her snugly. The sense of overwhelming vulnerability made Sarah want to cover up as much as possible. She removed the denim shirt from the bottom of her bag and slid it on, keeping it unbuttoned since it was actually too warm to wear it. She took out a travel-sized brush and began to untangle her hair. Little by little, the knots released—and her light brown hair was restored to its natural beauty.

Sarah felt much better. Enjoying the quiet, she took out her journal, made a place for herself on the small bed, and began to write.

I hardly know where to begin. I have found myself in a place only read about in fairy tales. I started out three days ago, thinking I would go on an adventure—and an adventure is sure what I got. Somehow, I entered into this other world. It looks as crazy on paper as it sounds in my head. I didn't believe this place or the small man named Tinbe was real, but the wounds on my legs from walking in the field earlier actually hurt. That stopped any thought I had that this might be a dream. It was very odd meeting Tinbe, but he has been a wonderful guide thus far. Although I have to admit I wonder why he is hesitant to tell me what this place is or why I am here. He has made mention of a man named Rika who I am to meet, and Tinbe says that he will explain everything to me. I sure hope he does because—although this place is beautiful and wondrous—he had fear in his eyes yesterday, and that fear has made its way into my heart.

Sarah closed the journal, put it back into her bag, and looked out of the small window which was centered on the main outside wall of the room. The triangle-shaped window was also decorated with beautiful wooden carvings. The plant on the sill was of the fern family, but she did not know what type.

The village was bustling with life, and everyone seemed to

be doing something. The same three youngsters were tending the booming fire in the pit. A woman in the middle of a team of children was reading something out of a tattered book. A pack of older children, perhaps teenagers, were playing some sort of game. The closest thing Sarah could relate it to was a cross between soccer and badminton. The coordination needed seemed impossible. She could not remember any kid she grew up with being quite that agile. A woman in a green dress caught Sarah's eye as she made her way across the center court and straight up the stairs to Sarah's room. When she knocked, Sarah went to the door and opened it.

She was a stout woman with skin that had many years of wear. Her silver hair was woven into the design of the village. She smiled at Sarah as she entered the room. "I hear your name be Sarah. I am Vente." She put some fresh linen on the edge of the bed, looked Sarah over from head to toe, and smiled again. "You will serve as a challenge to me, yes?"

"A challenge for what?" Sarah asked.

"My tailoring skill of course." Vente took out a long tape and began taking Sarah's measurements. "I am making sure of your size, as I believe you would say where you come from."

Sarah looked at her intently. "You know of where I come from?"

"Aye, but of course. Most of us do. It is just that only very few times in my life have I actually seen someone who crossed from where you would call home. I am very happy to make your acquaintance, Sarah. I hope you will be comfortable here. I hear you are on your way to meet with Rika."

"That's what Tinbe said. That's actually all Tinbe has said. I don't even know how I got here—or where here is—and all I'm being told is that it all will be explained to me when I meet with this Rika." Sarah sat at the edge of the bed and looked out the small window.

Vente looked at Sarah in the way a grandmother would look at her grandchild.

"Oh, Miss Sarah. You are but a young one, aren't you?" She walked over, placed her hand on Sarah's chin, and pulled her face up to look at hers. "You are confused and frightened? Come." She pulled Sarah up and finished taking her measurements. "You will come with me as I put this together, and we will talk. Food won't be ready for a while yet, and although I can tell you are tired, I can also tell you have more questions than answers. I will do what I can to remedy that." After pausing for a moment, Vente looked up at Sarah and said, "Although Rika would do better, I will do my best."

Sarah put her shoes on and followed Vente down the decorated staircase and past structures that overwhelmed her. When she went home, she would never look at trees the same way again. Sarah knew she probably wouldn't look at much of anything the same way again.

Vente walked slowly with Sarah. She explained how the people of Gropal had, over many generations, became very agile and moved about rather quickly.

The aroma in the courtyard was delightful for Sarah. The smells of meat and bread and open fire mixed together. Sarah hadn't eaten more than a few energy bars and Tinbe's stew. She was starved.

The whole scene had her spellbound. The village was

bustling. Sarah couldn't help but notice that every group of individuals she neared would stop what they were doing and smile. Some even bowed as she walked by. She knew she stuck out like a sore thumb; she was the only one over five feet tall and the only human in the bunch. She could not get over the bowing.

When they walked directly in front of the kids playing ball, they kept hitting the ball back and forth, but they gazed curiously at Sarah. She could not believe their dexterity and coordination—and they were smiling. She felt very welcome, almost like a celebrity.

Vente led her to a thick, incredibly designed door. It creaked as it swung open.

"This is one of our older homes." Vente giggled as she heard the squeak. "We notice things through a fresh perspective when company arrives. Please have a seat."

Vente was splendid and jolly in her nature—from the way she was dressed to the rosiness of her cheeks. As far as Sarah could tell, the people of the village had good lives. Quicker than she thought possible, she was growing to like her surroundings—as unusual as they might have been.

Vente gathered her fabric and said, "Now that I am here and you are here, what burdens your mind?"

"Well, first of all, where are we? What is the name of this place? Who are you? I mean your people?" Sarah had many more questions, but she was afraid she wouldn't be able to digest all the answers at once.

"We, my dear, are the people of Gropal. Some refer to us as Grinks." Vente made a sour face. "Our village was founded more than four hundred of your years ago by my father and his brother."

Sarah said, "Your *father*? How old was he when he died?"

Vente smiled. "He was 342, and to your understanding, my dear, that would make me 235 of your years." Turning to Sarah with a sweet smile, she added, "Not too shabby for my age, yes?"

Sarah wanted to know how that was possible, but there were other things she needed to know first. "How is it that I got here?" Sarah thought that was an easy enough question.

Vente came over to Sarah, sat down in the chair across from her, and continued sewing. "The best I have been able to explain it, my dear, is that you had a desire in your heart when you entered the opening. Rika will be able to explain that part a bit better than I can. Tinbe tells me that he found you asleep under the great tree—smack in the middle of Hofflinar."

"That's what he told me," Sarah exclaimed. "But what is Hofflinar?"

Vente stopped sewing and concentrated on Sarah's face. "Hofflinar is the place that the wicked of our world go to rest. Tinbe and I are unsure of how it was you came into our world from that place. He had gone on his yearly journey there to make sure all was the same as the year before when he came across you. The openings to our world are sporadic, yes? We are just very pleased that you weren't let out in the Dark Land. If you had been, you would have been dead long before any one of us even knew you were here, especially without a guide." She slapped her leg and stood up, still holding her fabric. "But that was not the way of it, and here you are."

She pulled Sarah over to a small stool, pinned the fabric, and began to sew again.

Sarah digested the information and watched in amazement as Vente put together the seams. Sarah couldn't sew at all, and she was even more impressed than she might have been otherwise.

As it went down, the sun peeked through the long window at the opposite side of the room. The beams hit the fabric that, with Vente's touch, lay perfectly on Sarah.

Vente said, "There. I believe it's one of my finest efforts. Come and see."

She led Sarah over to what would probably have been considered a full-length mirror to the people of Gropal. Sarah was able to see herself well enough to be impressed by the simplistic beauty of the dress. It was dark ivory and draped on her perfectly. Its length was centered perfectly on her calf, the sleeves came to just below her wrists, which Sarah liked very much, and the neckline was low enough to let her breathe without being indecent. What amazed her even more than the perfect fit were the stitches that kept the garment together. They were made of the same material as all the ropes she had seen. Intertwined was the sparkling hint of a silvery material that gave the dress a look and feel of simple elegance.

"It's ... beautiful," Sarah said softly.

"As you are, my dear," Vente replied with a warm smile.

A bell sounded, and Vente clapped her hands. "Just in time too. Our other guests have arrived, which means food is done too. Let's go."

Sarah took another look in the mirror and followed Vente down to the courtyard.

ఐ Chapter 3

ALL THE ACTION HAD DIED DOWN, AND ALMOST EVERYONE was seated on makeshift cushions around the fire. They were all so preoccupied with their conversations that Sarah made it almost all the way to the cushion that had been reserved for her before they noticed. Then, in unison, everyone stopped talking. All eyes were on her and Vente.

Vente motioned for Sarah to take her place, and after Sarah sat down, an older man stood, raised his goblet, and said, "Here we have a most unusual guest. One who most of our young have only heard of in their bedtime tales." He motioned to Sarah.

The group interrupted the toast with a round of applause.

The man continued, "Her name is Sarah. She has come to us from beyond our border with a dream in her heart. That dream, of what is yet to be seen, was what opened our doors. So as our land opened its doors to her, we shall open our hearts." He raised his goblet higher, and all followed suit. When he said, "Eat," they did.

Sarah took great delight in the food that was presented to her. The meat was cooked perfectly, and the breads and vegetables were better than she had ever tasted. She ate until she was full and then sat back and watched.

Across the way, she saw Tinbe for the first time since he had settled her into her room. He was looking right at her, and when their eyes met, he gave her a comforting smile and a sly wink.

Sarah leaned over to Vente and said, "Who are the guests you mentioned … besides me, I mean?"

Vente finished chewing, took a sip from her goblet, and smiled. "Ah, he is here and will choose when to make himself known."

A soft horn blew, almost like an afterthought, and everyone around the fire stood.

Sarah couldn't see what they were looking at until a tall man walked out from the shadows. His wavy brown hair framed his strong features nicely. He was dressed like a woodsman, but his demeanor was that of a prince. His eyes were as blue as the sea after a storm, and they were staring right at her.

The old man who had made the toast bowed low and said, "We all welcome you, Taurik, to our feast. Sit and enjoy."

The crowd burst into applause again.

Without taking his eyes off Sarah, Taurik made his way over to the seat that had been left vacant next to her. He took Sarah's hand, kissed it gently, and motioned for her to sit with him. "Word had it that you were beautiful, but no one told me that you would steal my very breath."

His smile melted Sarah. She said, "You flatter me, sir. Thank you. May I ask who you are and how you heard of me?"

"You may. But first, I will eat. Then if it pleases you, we will walk together. And then you and I may talk the night through, if you wish."

Sarah really just wanted sleep, but the temptation to know this man was far too great. She drank another goblet of punch as she waited for Taurik to finish.

Vente and Tinbe came over to Sarah. As Tinbe put his hand on her back, Vente leaned closer to her and said, "You are safe with him, my dear. Talk with him. Have a good night. We will be awaiting your next move in the morning."

Before Sarah could say anything, Tinbe, Vente, and many of the others went back to their homes. One by one, the lights in the surrounding cabins went dim and then out.

Sarah and Taurik were left alone, looking into the fire together.

After some time, when all was quiet, Taurik said, "I am Taurik, son of Rika. Do you know why you are here? Better yet," he said with a smile, "do you know why *I* am here?"

"I am afraid I can't answer many questions. I only know what I have been told so far, and I am sorry to say that isn't much. Although it is obvious I am safe here," Sarah answered while looking into the flames.

"Yes, it is true that here you are safe," Taurik said. "There are those in this land, though, who would hurt you. That is why my father has sent me here. I am to be your guide to the Highlands of Eslinar, the land of my people, and there you will meet with my father Rika, and then—"

"Then he will explain. Yes, I know." Sarah stood and walked away.

Taurik quickly finished his goblet and came after her.

"What is it, Sarah?" He grabbed her by the shoulders, making her stop.

"Ever since I got here, that's all I've been told that Rika will explain everything. There are some things I can figure out all by myself, you know?" she said sarcastically. "I can figure out that I have crossed some sort of threshold that folks refer to as the border. I can figure out that, until I met you, I was the only one who even looked human. And I can figure out that no one here is willing to tell me how the hell it all happened—or why I am here in the first place." She began to shake and cry. The many days of unbelievable happenings all came to a point in her psyche, and she could no longer keep her strong face on.

Taurik took her into his arms and held on tightly.

She finally let herself go and emptied her heart of fear onto his strong shoulder.

"Sarah, listen now. You are safe still, and I will do all that I can to help you find your meaning here. You are the light that many of us seek—and the light that some want to stop. Either way, none of that is of importance at this moment." He gently pulled her off him, and she looked into his eyes. She believed him.

He walked her back to her cabin and said, "I will come for you in the morning. Rest now and know that you are safe. I won't be far. If you need me, just think it. Good night." With a kiss to her forehead, he turned—and she was alone.

All Sarah wanted at that moment was to sleep, but sleep was harder to come by than it should have been. She got out of the dress and draped it over the back of an armchair in the corner. She brushed her hair and thought about losing her cool in front of Taurik. Almost every part of her felt bad except one. That part of her understood that the past few days would have broken anyone she knew back home. Sarah thought about her home, her job, and her mother. She did not want anyone to be worried, but she had only been gone a few days, and no one would be expecting her back for another month.

She crawled into the soft bed, and her journal caught her attention. She decided that the only way to get her mind to quiet down enough for sleep was to get out some of the thoughts roaming around in it. She sat up, got the journal, and opened to the next available page.

I began this day with one state of mind, but now I have another altogether. I was introduced to a lady named Vente today. She took good care of me and helped ease some of my worries. But still, she was not able to answer any of my questions regarding my purpose here. She said that Rika could answer those types of questions much better than she could. She made me clothes that, to my amazement, look really good on me. Her talent is second to none. Dinner was very nice. It was around a large fire, but something did pull at my heart a bit. The old man making the toast referred to me as "something the little ones heard of in nighttime tales." What did he mean by that? Who do these people think I am? I have so many questions. I met the most beautiful man I think I have ever encountered. His name is Taurik. He says he is the son of Rika and that he has come to guide me to his father in safety. People here keep reminding me I am safe, and even though it does comfort parts of me, it also opens more questions. From what— or from whom—am I safe?

Sarah closed the journal and fell into a deep, dreamless sleep.

Vente, Tinbe, the Elder Binate, and Taurik entered Binate's parlor. As they gathered around the cobblestone fireplace, Binate called for his servant to bring them all hot tea. Each one asked for it the way he or she liked, and they were pleased when they got to sit back in their seats and enjoy the warmth of the tea.

The room was only illuminated by the fire and a few candles on either end of the room. The furniture was draped in finely decorated red fabric, and the furniture was made out of beautifully carved wood. The room was big enough to hold many more people, but only that many would be comfortable sitting around the fire.

Binate said, "I have asked you all here to tell me what you know thus far about our guest. She is obviously human. She's very beautiful and quite young. What I want to know is what isn't so obvious. I would like to hear your observations." He paused for a moment. "I want to know what you saw that plain sight could not see." He sat back, took a long sip of his tea, and waited a moment.

Vente said, "If you mean do I think she is the one with light, my answer would have to be yes. She is so beautiful. That much is obvious. Quite right, quite right." After taking a short sip from her mug, she continued, "She was unusually polite even through what she must be feeling. The sense I was picking up was that of intrigue and a bit of fear, but I suppose that's to be expected at this point. I felt no dark forces in her—that much I know." Vente sat back.

Tinbe leaned forward in his chair and cleared his throat. "To me, pleasant she was. Hungry, tired, confused mostly was she. Her light led me to her, it did, in that dark place. Aye, yes, good is she." He sat back and looked at all present before he took a sip of his tea.

They all looked to Taurik. He stood and walked over to the window. Gazing outside and over to her room, he said, "She is the one of light. She will cast a shadow on all that come against her, but ..."

Binate turned in his seat slightly and looked at Taurik. "Go on, lad. What is it that's on your mind?"

"It's not what is in my mind but in my heart," Taurik said in a low voice. "Although she is filled with the light we were waiting for, I am unsure if she is strong enough." He turned from the window and reclaimed his chair next to the fire.

Binate lit his pipe and said, "That, Sir Taurik, would be the end of us all. Let's hope you are wrong."

Before he could go any further, Vente said, "Not strong enough? How? Her spirit is filled with dreams, hopes, and desire. How could that be seen as weak?"

Taurik replied, "Her spirit is not what worries me. It is her mind. It is clouded by doubt and fear. But, Vente, you are right about her spirit. I just hope she will be able to find it before her mind and her desires are found and tempted."

The morning came slowly as the sun crept over the horizon. Birds began to sing outside of Sarah's window, and as slowly as the sun, she arose out of bed. Wiping the sleep from her eyes, she had to take a minute to remember where she was. She was not frightened, but she was anxious about what would happen next. Who would she meet? What would they be like? Then she remembered Taurik—and his eyes, his touch, and his voice reminding her that she was safe and he was to be her guide. Sarah knew he would help her no matter what happened next.

With a renewed faith, Sarah got out of bed and put on the dress and sandals. The day was hot already, and although the dress breathed well enough, the back of her neck was uncomfortably hot. Tying her hair back and checking herself in the mirror, Sarah closed the door behind her. Taking in a deep breath, she went down the stairs with a spring in her step, ready to face the day.

Taurik was there to meet her as he said he would be, and they ate breakfast with the whole village around the fire pit.

"Miss Sarah," Taurik said, "I hope you don't find this too bold of me, but may I say that you look radiant this morning. You are feeling better, I take it?"

"I slept great … if that's what you mean," she said with a giggle and a smile. "I am feeling a little better, yes. You did me a great service by letting me tell you how I was really feeling inside. I will admit I am still a little scared about not knowing what this place is and why I am here, but a journey is what I wanted. As they say where I come from, 'Be careful what you wish for.'" She smiled and turned away with a slight blush as he returned the smile.

"We leave for Eslinar after we are finished here. Are you ready?" Taurik asked.

"I am as ready as I can be with all the mystery surrounding this journey of ours." She smiled gently. "No time like the present. I'll go get my things." She bounced up to her cabin and gathered her belongings. She was mindful to pack her journal and first-aid kit, but it was too cumbersome to bring more than a denim bottom and a T-shirt or two. She left behind the mangled items of clothing in a small pile at the end of the bed.

Taurik, Tinbe, Vente, and the Elder Binate were waiting for her by the fire pit.

They all looked concerned.

Vente approached Sarah with a trinket in her hand. She held it out to Sarah and said, "This is a medallion made of wood and the tears of falcons. Handcrafted so long ago, the stories of it are faint. It is meant to protect the one who carries it. It saved the life of my father once. I hope that you will not need it—but take it. It is yours now." She handed the medallion to Sarah, gave her a hug, and stepped aside.

Tinbe stepped up to Sarah and gave her a gentle smile. "See you go, I do not want, but you must. Give you, I will, my trusty pot. Meals of many out of it have I, and hungry you should go never." He handed the pot to her, touched her arm, and stepped aside.

Binate took his place in front of Sarah and said, "I am Binate. We meet formally only as you leave. This I do regret. If your destiny is as we hope, I will have time later to sit with you, if you will allow?"

Sarah returned his thoughtful look. "I would like that very much, Binate. I don't know what my destiny is either, but I am excited to find out." She giggled nervously.

Binate reached into his golden cloak. "This I give you because I believe you are the one for it." He lifted a small plain goblet which had no design but was scuffed and dented on all of its surface. "If you are the one, the purest waters will open up so you will drink from them. Only this goblet will take that water to your lips. Safe journey to you, Sarah." Binate walked back to his cabin.

Taurik said, "You are ready then?"

Sarah was trying to make sense of the riddles, but she realized things would all be answered if she gave them enough time. She put her new possessions into her backpack, looked at Taurik, and said, "If you are?"

Sarah was excited to leave the village, but as the day dragged on, they never left the canopy of trees. "Can we stop for a few?" Sarah called to Taurik who was about four paces in front of her.

"Almost," he said. "We need to make it over that rise first. Then we will put up camp for the night, and you can rest all you like." Taurik walked briskly and didn't turn toward her.

The rise didn't look all that far away, and Sarah concentrated on other things besides her bodily functions and fatigue. The surrounding trees grew in size as they went. The canopy grew thicker, and the underbrush grew thinner.

Sarah guessed it was from the lack of sun until she saw part of it move. With a yelp, she called out, "What was that?"

Taurik grabbed her hand and yelled, "Run, Sarah! We are almost at the rise. We must get there!"

The ground beneath them grew more violent with every few strides. Sarah ran as fast as her aching feet would take her, which was almost as fast as Taurik was pulling her. The underbrush began to fly into the air, clumps at a time, and a howl reverberated in their ears.

Sarah began to slow with weariness.

"Come on!" Taurik yelled. "Look out for the Jagruts!"

Something crashed just behind them. It looked like a large tree root smacking the ground. The whole scene became all too real for Sarah when one of the roots lifted the ground and threw her into the air. She flew over Taurik's head and smashed on the ground like a rag doll.

Taurik ran to her, opened her bag, and took out Vente's medallion. Sarah was unconscious. She had landed on top of a very thick bush. As long as her feet were not touching the surface, the attackers could not detect her easily.

Taurik tried to revive Sarah, hoping she was not seriously injured. It was only a matter of minutes before the creatures would catch her scent and attack again.

"Wake up, Sarah! Please!" He held the medallion in one hand and her head in the other. "You have to wake up now—or we will both surely die! Sarah, wake—"

A large Jagrut shifted the earth below them and came rising up only feet away. It shadowed them with its massiveness.

Sarah began to stir, and as she opened her eyes, she let out a bloodcurdling scream.

"Hold this!" Taurik said quickly. "Say it loud … *telgot de nomtera!*"

Sarah grabbed the medallion and yelled, *"Telgot de nomtera!"*

The massive Jagrut made a screeching growl that pierced their ears like a hot dagger as it sank back into the ground.

Sarah grabbed Tuarik's hand. After he helped her to her feet, they continued on with vivacity and without another complaint.

Just before nightfall, they came across the rise. Taurik pointed to a small piece of land in the middle of a flowing stream. Putting down his satchel, he climbed a nearby tree. Within a few minutes, he had cut off a large enough limb to cross over to the island. He kicked away the limb and said, "Are you all right?"

Physically shaken—and getting stiffer by the minute—Sarah answered, "As all right as anyone would be after being attacked by a tree." Sarcasm had been a tool of Sarah's for most of her life. At that moment, the sarcasm in her voice was unavoidable, and so was the utter lack of accompanying smiles.

Taurik took Sarah's bag from her shoulder and put it down. "Gather yourself while I get some wood—and then we will eat." He turned and went out into the sparse landscape.

Sarah's body was asking her for relief and fuel. Both things were battling with her fatigue. Mother Nature won out, and Sarah ventured far enough into the brush to where she felt private. After she was done, she came back and began to unpack her blanket roll, which had been tied to the underbelly of her pack. She remembered what Tinbe had done with the leaves and did her best to mimic it so she could have some comfort.

When Taurik came back, his arms were filled with all sizes of wood. When a fire was made, he sat down across from Sarah and said, "Most people wouldn't have lived through that back there."

"What was that back there anyway? And what's the deal with this medallion?" She was clenching it in her fist so hard that part of the design was left imprinted on her hand.

"That, Miss Sarah, was a Jagrut—and quite a large one at that." He took out a bowl from his satchel and filled it with water from his canister and some herbs from a pouch. Placing the bowl on the fire, he continued, "The Jagruts thrive in the lands between the Dark City and Gropal. They usually attack and eat without discrimination. It seemed to have a target this time, but usually Gropal is indirectly protected by the Jagruts, so we let them be. Everything has a purpose, although it can be hard to see at times."

"If they eat," Sarah said with a shiver, "anything that passes, why did we come this way? Isn't there another way around?" She couldn't believe the danger she had been in. Never in her life had she come so close to death. Her head had begun to swell slightly from the collision with the earth, and her hair was sticky in a small spot at the top of her neck from blood.

"The only other way around is more hazardous, and it takes much longer to cross." Taurik took out two small bowls, filled them with broth, and passed one to Sarah.

She took it eagerly and began to calm down. Most of her nerves were quieted, but her head throbbed from injury and fatigue.

Taurik said, "I know this world is not like the one you lived in, but I assure you that it is all very real. I am here to help." Taurik began to inspect her injuries. "You must trust me, Sarah, but more than that or anything else, you must trust this." He pointed to the center of her chest.

Sarah looked at him with vulnerability.

Taurik put some ointment on the back of her head and said, "I see you've made yourself a nice resting place."

"It's a trick I learned from Tinbe the night after he found me." She lay down on top of the blanket.

Taurik covered her with his cloak. "Rest now, Miss Sarah. You will need your strength tomorrow, but for now, you are safe."

Sarah hung the medallion around her neck and closed her eyes. She drifted off to sleep, listening to the serene sounds of the forest.

Taurik looked at Sarah intently for a long while. Her hair was dangling about her peaceful face, her beautiful eyes were hidden by her long-lashed lids, and her mouth parted just enough for her shallow breaths. She looked like an angel.

Taurik's father had told him of Sarah many years earlier during his training. He had been told that she would be lovely and that only one of such loveliness could carry a light so great that it would save his world from ruin. He hoped she would be able to bear the burden when it was her time.

Taurik's world was riddled with forces of good and evil,

much like the world Sarah came from. In Sarah's world, good and evil would do battle in conflicts between nations or crimes against one another, almost always for selfish gains. In his world, good and evil's battleground centered in the mind, body, and spirit. A person's true nature would find itself and grow. Personal truth determined good and evil, and for those who found it, their paths were set. Unlike good, evil would trick, manipulate, and place fear in the hearts of those it wanted to overtake. The only real difference between the two was that in Taurik's world, a person's path was visible to everyone else.

Rika had tried to draw parallels for Taurik throughout his training so he could understand Sarah's perception of others. Taurik's duty was to guide Sarah through the internal chaos her journey would invoke. He only hoped that the frail angel in front of the fire would have enough courage.

Taurik knew the journey through one's own soul was long and hard, and without courage, strength, determination, and a strong sense of self, the forces of darkness would overcome.

Many of the Dark Land's tenants had once been like Taurik. Others had been kind and generous like the people of Gropal. All of them were quick with weapons, talented in crafts, and had much wisdom, but they were taken by their own darkness and never returned. They became broken creatures with nothing left but the need for bedlam and a blind devotion to the one who guided the madness. They were also taught, after falling to evil, that above all else, death must come to the one who carried the true light: Sarah. They thought of no one but themselves and cared not what happened to the world they once knew—if any of them remembered it at all.

Taurik knew Sarah was going to need much support to get through the Dark Land in one piece. The Dark Lord also knew of her arrival and had passed down a decree to all that inhabited his lands that she was to be stopped by any means necessary. If she found out who she really was, the Dark Lord would lose his grip on his land and all that served him.

Looking again at Sarah, Taurik smiled. Although he feared for her, he also felt a strong faith. He began to see strength in her that she was not yet aware of. Taurik rested his head on his satchel. Any rest he could get would be better than none. He knew he would need his strength too if he was to be her aid.

They had only one day to pass through the land ahead of them. He thought he could push it to two, but Sarah would need rest and nourishment on a regular basis. Contrary to what he'd been taught, Taurik knew they would not be able to stop once they started.

He drifted off with hope in his heart, reminding himself that he too was safe.

❧ Chapter 4

MORNING CAME AS SLOWLY AS THE NIGHT HAD FALLEN, AND one sound at a time, life returned to the little island. Taurik arose first and started gathering wood for the fire. Sarah gradually started to stir when she heard his movements.

Breakfast was delightful. Sarah didn't know how Taurik could make such a delicious meal with so few ingredients over a small, open fire like that. She was impressed. Taurik explained how they only had two days at most, preferably one, to cross the Dark Land—and it was imperative not to stop for anything.

Sarah was getting used to the mysterious nature of the place, but she had a question. "Why can't we stop?" she said as she stuffed another bundle of food in her mouth.

"If we do, we will die." He finished chewing his food and looked up at Sarah.

"What do you mean by that?" Sarah asked.

"I mean just what I said." He put down his plate, took out a rag, and began cleaning up. "In the Dark Land, outsiders are considered prey and are free for the taking. Usually that would mean certain and quick death, but you are not a normal outsider. The Dark Lord has told of your arrival to his tenants so you can be assured that you will be hunted from the moment we begin until the moment we cross the outer boundary into Eslinar. Either way, it is not good if we stop." He began to pack up his satchel. "As long as we keep moving, they will not be able to get a lock on either of us." As he tied the lip of his bag, he looked over to Sarah with a seriousness she had not seen before. "I do not know if even I will be able to predict the trials that lay ahead of you. Nor do I know if I will be able to fully protect or even prepare you for them. I can tell you only that our best chance to make it to the other side is to not stop." He stood up and started to put out the fire.

"Taurik, what does this Dark Lord want with me? I don't even know how I got here, much less what I'm actually doing here. Everyone here seems to know me better than I do." She finished packing her bag, stood, and met his stare. "How am I supposed to keep moving for that long?"

Taurik walked over and said, "I don't know, Sarah. I wish I did." He took her by the shoulders like he had the first night. "I can offer you no more answers. This is your journey, your fight. It's about you, Sarah. I can only help guide you. I will give you some advice. Keep true to yourself, trust yourself, and stay swift. Do you understand?"

Sarah looked up into his blue eyes and said, "I'll try." Stepping back from him, she put her pack on and motioned for him to go first.

The distance between that side of the island and the opposite shore was much greater than the river they had crossed the night before. At first, Taurik looked concerned, but he rigged up a crossing in no time with a large trunk he found and a line of rope, which he threw to the other side. The rope wrapped around a branch of a tree, and as he crossed, he used it to steady himself. Once he was across, he tossed the rope back to Sarah.

With a deep breath, she started across.

Taurik made it look easy as he glided across the log.

When Sarah began, she couldn't help but notice that the water was about fifteen feet below her and was rushing past her a lot faster than she had previously noticed. She held on to the rope, put her foot out onto the log, and slowly pulled herself up.

"Look at me!" Taurik shouted over the rushing water. "Sarah, don't look at the log. Hold the rope. Look at me. Put one foot in front of the other!"

Sarah could only nod to his commands and did her best to comply with them. The well-fitted sandals Vente had made her allowed her to feel her way. She was moving along well, but when she reached the center of the log, the winds picked up and the water began to rise. Sarah lost her grip and fell, clutching the log to her breast. The wind was knocked from her, but she held on to the log and to the rope with all her strength.

"Sarah!" Taurik shouted as he jumped toward the edge. He started to tie the rope around his waist so he could go after her, but he looked up and Sarah was on her feet.

Sarah looked into Taurik's eyes and began to walk again. She gripped the rope and made her way to the shore.

Once on land, Taurik took the rope from around her waist and coiled it around his shoulder. No words were spoken between them, but Sarah smiled.

"Ready?" Taurik asked.

"Not much of a welcome. Was it?" She tried to deflate the looming tension with a little humor, and Taurik bought into it for a second.

"Well, are you?" Taurik asked again with a chuckle.

"I suppose. But if this is the kind of hospitality these people show at the door, I can't wait for the main course." She smiled at Taurik, but when she looked at him, he was not smiling anymore.

"Yes, you can. Come. I will set the pace, and once it's set, you must keep it."

Taurik started off a bit too quickly for Sarah, but before long, their pace matched. Through the dense trees that were looming with shadows, they made their way over and through the underbrush. The swift pace was good for longer than Taurik had planned, but Sarah began to fade gradually. As she slowed, she started to hear rustling in the brush all around them.

"Move, Sarah! You must move!" Taurik yelled.

Sarah picked up the pace as much as she could, but her heart was beating heavily in her chest. The more she tried to concentrate on something else, the more the sound of her pulse reverberated in her ears. Her breath was becoming erratic, and she yelled, "We ... have ... to ... slow ... down!"

They had been running for long while and they had barely covered the needed distance. They needed to keep going, but Sarah could not.

Taurik also heard the rustling around them, but he knew what it was. He was not looking forward to what came next. Taurik would have to fight them off as Sarah caught her breath. It was the only way, and he knew it. If she lost consciousness, it would mean certain death for them both.

Sarah's running turned into a trot and then to a walk, and then she buckled over. She held her head down low with her hands on her knees to give her some support.

Taurik drew his weapon and stood between her and the rustling brush. The noise grew louder and louder until it was right on top of them, and then it was still. Taurik said, "Is the medallion on your neck?"

Gasping for breath in between coughs, she answered, "Yes."

"I will hold them off as long as I can! Get your breath as fast as you can! When you can, run!"

As he said that, a beast jumped out at him like a rock launched from a slingshot. Taurik was thrown back, but he quickly regained his footing. He swung with the might of a warrior at the beast. Slashed by Taurik's blade, the beast let out an outrageous scream and fell. Another came from his right. Taurik's sword penetrated through the creases of its scales, and that one too fell. The attack continued for some time, but Taurik boldly stood between the scaly creatures and Sarah.

One of the creatures came at Sarah while Taurik was busy fighting another. She saw its mouth open, and its teeth were as sharp as a great white shark. Sarah let out a bloodcurdling scream as she was tackled, but Taurik thrust his dagger deep into the attacker's back. As it tried to get up, Taurik pushed the blade in deeper. Blood streamed out of the cracks in the scales, and the creature fell to the ground.

Taurik grabbed Sarah by the wrist and pulled her to

her feet. "Can you go on?" With nothing more than an acknowledging nod, they were off again.

The terrain was unforgiving; the inclines were steeper, and the rocks underfoot were larger. Sarah caught her breath, and incredible fear pushed her on. Sarah could not rid herself of the gray scales, the foaming mouths, or the bloodlust in the creatures' eyes.

"We have made it more than halfway, Sarah!" Taurik yelled as he tied a rope around the limb of a large tree at the edge of a cliff.

"What are you doing?" Sarah yelled.

Thundering sounds were coming from behind them. "We must get down into the valley! It's the only way!" He was concentrating so much on securing the rope that he didn't notice Sarah's pale skin.

"Climb down?" Sarah looked over the edge and saw how far they were from the bottom. Her knees began to shake, and when she looked behind her, she saw an army of the scaly creatures coming straight for them.

Taurik quickly tied the rope around them, and before Sarah could say or think anything, he flung them both over the edge of the cliff.

Sarah screamed and clung to Taurik, and faster than she thought possible, the rope went taut. The stop was not very pleasant—they smashed into the rock face—but at least they were alive.

They dangled for a moment before the creatures began to tug at the rope.

Sarah yelled, "They're pulling us up!"

"I'm just glad they don't have the sense to cut it." Taurik looked up to the top and then down below.

One inch at a time, the pair was being pulled back to the top of the cliff.

Sarah screamed.

"Look up." Taurik pointed to a ledge about five feet above them. "We are lucky we didn't hit it on the way down, but it will do nicely for now—and they are doing the work for us."

Still dangling from the rope, Taurik smiled at Sarah. She felt comforted in the midst of chaos. They reached the ledge, and he helped her onto it. He followed, untying the rope from around their waists quickly.

"Get up as close to the side as you can. They can't see you there," Taurik said.

Sarah had a chance to look out over the land in front of them. She saw the tops of amazing structures that peeked out through the trees. To their left, a magnificent waterfall was covered with a rainbow from the sun hitting its mist. To their right, there was a vast field. Closer to them, the land was covered in a hazy shadow, and she could not make out any details.

"Get back!" Taurik said.

A rock came down hard—right where Sarah had been leaning out—and another followed it. Taurik was shocked when the next thing to land was one of the scaled soldiers. It flew over the edge and landed at the edge of the cliff, barely missing it.

The rope began to fall, and Taurik caught it. Tossing it quickly to the side, he threw himself between the creature and Sarah. The greenish-gray creature was stunned by the impact, but after a moment, it shook itself off and knelt in front of them silently. He was half the size of the creatures that had attacked them in the woods, but he was still quite robust.

Sarah watched for any movement underneath its scaly armor. The young creature's thick, black hair hung over his shoulder in a tight braid. His eyes were as dark as his hair, and he was looking straight at them. Slowly, he started to rise. Stopping halfway up, he grabbed his side. Despite the pain, he stood tall.

"Throw down your weapon!" Taurik said.

The creature stood slowly, unlatched the buckle on his belt, and threw it to the ground at Taurik's feet. A knife with a jagged edge clanked as it hit the surface.

Sarah reached down and grabbed it—along with the belt—and quickly tied it around her waist. It was too big, but she wrapped it twice so it wouldn't fall off.

The creature began to unbuckle his armor methodically. Taurik's stance relaxed as the creature unveiled himself to them. His neck was long, and his shoulders were lean. His chest was much lankier without the armor.

The noise from above quieted as the herd of creatures disbanded. When the three of them were standing silent and alone, Sarah silently thanked God that the ledge was as big as it was.

The creature pointed to himself with a stubby finger and bowed his head. "I am Sar, son of Nib."

Taurik held out his blade. "Taurik, son of Rika."

From behind Taurik, Sarah said, "I am Sarah." Feeling a little safer, she took one step to the side.

Sar looked at her, and his eyes filled with wonder. He took one step closer, knelt on one knee, and said in a soft voice, "You are she." He bowed his head again, stood up, and went back to his original position. He looked at Taurik and said, "There are only few of us who believe Sarah is good. It was not a mistake that I am here with you, although it was almost my death." He looked back over his shoulder to the ground, many hundreds of feet below, and took a step away from the edge.

"Have we reason to trust you?" Taurik said, raising his blade again as he moved.

Sarah noticed his hostile motion. She reached out and touched his shoulder. "I think we can, Taurik." Her eyes met Sar's. "I don't see any hate in his eyes. Do you?" She motioned for Taurik to look, and Taurik agreed that Sar was not a threat. Taurik returned his blade to his hip.

The sun was setting quickly, and Taurik started to unpack his satchel.

Sarah began to unpack her bag, and Sar began to tear apart his armor. "Why are you doing that?" Sarah asked.

"It will be dark and cold soon," Sar said. "We need to stay warm, and my armor will be good for fire. I will not be needing it anymore."

Soon the fire was going, and Sarah was surprised by how long one piece of armor could burn. She remembered the pot that Tinbe had given her and reached into her bag for it. She handed it over to Taurik with a smile. "I don't know what he meant by it, but he said that I wouldn't go hungry. I guess I'll have to tell him to get it fixed because I'm famished." As soon she finished talking, the pot felt heavier. She looked inside and was astounded to find that it had filled with a thick porridge. It was tasty and satisfied all of their stomachs. With full bellies and heavy minds, they looked into the fire and up at the stars.

Sarah asked, "You said that it wasn't a mistake that you are here. What did you mean by that?"

Sar looked up into the sky, then over to Taurik and Sarah, and replied, "Legend has said for as long as I can remember, and as far back in history as my father's father, that another from beyond would come and return our world to us. That not all who would come to us were like those who had come before. That when the good returned, so would the glory of this world—and with it, my people." He looked down at the fire and his burning armor. "There are not many of us left who long for a time like that. Most of my people have fallen too far, and the ones who remain have to hide our trueness to survive."

He shivered a bit when a cool breeze whirled past them.

Sarah took the denim shirt from her bag and put it around Sar's shoulders.

Sar continued, "My father, my uncle, and I had heard of your arrival, as did everyone else. It didn't take long before the Lord of the Dark had petitioned to us all that a heavy bounty would be paid for anyone who brought you to him, and that in addition to the bounty, all their lands for generations to come would only have to slave for him half of what they do now."

Taurik said, "You were not tempted by this offer?"

"My family and I were tempted, yes, I will admit to that. But the greater good of all my people, including my family, depends on the success of your quest." He looked at Sarah, and his black eyes put forth softness.

"You two get some rest." Taurik propped himself against the wall. "I will keep watch for tonight." He looked to Sarah and smiled. "Sleep, Sarah. For tomorrow, we will have more to do."

Sar had already begun to rest. He was no longer cold, but his chest was starting to bruise from the impact earlier.

Sarah said, "Taurik, we will have to take a look at his wound in the morning, okay?"

Taurik nodded and stirred the fire a bit.

Sarah rested her head on her bag, which was growing more comfortable with each passing night. Watching the red ash rise from the fire into the night sky, her body began to relax; she fell asleep quickly.

Taurik watched Sarah sleep for some time. He was amazed by her grace, and she was so unaware of it. She didn't know she was beautiful or understand the goodness of her own heart. He hoped she would find what her heart's desire was, and he could not help but wonder if he would play any part in it.

He looked over toward Sar, and for the first time, he saw what Sarah saw when she looked at him. He did not see the threat from before. He saw only a thin boy with scars on his back and arms. Sar must have lived a brutal existence. Taurik couldn't help but wonder how any good could have survived in such an evil environment. He was uncertain of Sar's role in Sarah's quest, but he knew he was not the one to judge that. His father told him before he left for Gropal that he must not interfere in matters other than Sarah's bodily protection. Regardless of the outcome, he was to be her guide and protector—and that was it. Taurik leaned against the cliff's face and put a bundle from his satchel behind his head. He checked that his weapons were near and fell asleep while listening to the sounds around them.

When the sun rose, Sar was the first to awake. He quietly restarted the fire with another piece of his armor. When he reached for the rope, Taurik grabbed his wrist and said, "What are you doing?"

"I have spotted a way down from here," he answered calmly.

Taurik remembered the boy he saw sleeping by the fire the night before and slowly let go of Sar's wrist. He said, "Before we do that, let's have a look at your side." He moved his satchel and reached inside. Pulling out a bandage, he stood Sar up and began wrapping his ribs.

"I feel foolish for mistrusting you," Taurik said in a low voice.

"You had—and still have—no reason to trust me." Sar looked right at Taurik. "My people are cruel, and their legacy is one of torture and war … even to their own people."

Taurik nodded.

Sarah coughed as she sat up and with all the energy she could muster at that hour. "Should we eat before we try to get off this rock?" She smiled, but she just wanted to keep her mind off their predicament.

Taurik and Sar smiled to each other and joined Sarah around the fire to enjoy another serving of the magic stew from Tinbe's pot.

"So what's your idea for getting off this rock?" Taurik asked Sar.

Sar pointed over Taurik's shoulder. "Over on that side, jagged edges span the whole the face, as far as I can see."

"How far can you see?" Sarah asked, looking up at him before she filled her mouth with soup.

"I can see just short of the bottom," he said.

"How short?" Taurik asked.

Sar finished his bowl and looked at them both. "I will admit to you that I cannot see all the way down, but I searched around for a better spot and found none. The rest of the edges are sheer as glass."

Instead of leaning over the edge to confirm Sar's findings, Sarah began to pack up her things and extinguished the fire. She handed Sar a tightly wrapped bundle. It contained the remainder of his armor. "I thought these might come in handy later on," she said.

Sar nodded but was distracted as he watched Taurik go from edge to edge.

Taurik said, "He's right. It is the only way down from here." He threw Sar the rope and watched with Sarah as Sar wrapped it around a piece of rock that stuck out from the cliff.

Taurik tested the knot, and it didn't move from its spot or show any signs of unraveling.

Feeling a bit nervous, Sarah asked, "Who goes first?"

"I will," Sar said, looking at Taurik and Sarah with boldness in his eyes.

Sar started to slowly rappel, and Taurik said, "Sarah, you go next."

"No," Sarah said. "I don't know if I can do this, Taurik."

"Sarah, you must. We must get off this rock. It's not safe here any longer. We must move." He took one step toward her and gently touched his lips to her forehead. "You can do this, Sarah. Your strength runs deeper than you think. Have faith."

After an understanding glance between the two of them, Sarah slowly made her way to the edge and reached for the rope. Looking down, she could see Sar rappelling at an incredible rate. He seemed agile and experienced. She started to giggle; nothing like that would have been on her to-do list at home. The thought of home made her momentarily sad, but before the thought could complete itself, Taurik touched her shoulder.

"Ready?" he said gently.

She nodded and stepped out onto the rock face, holding the rope as tightly as she could.

Taurik coached her for a minute or two until she got the hang of it. Then he joined them on the rope, and the three of them rappelled toward the bottom.

Taurik slowed his pace to match Sarah's. If he rushed her, she would tire more quickly.

Sar was far beneath them. When he saw Taurik and Sarah stop, he shouted, "We will make it!"

Taurik looked down to Sar.

"The bottom is near, and we have enough rope!" Sar shouted.

Taurik said, "Sarah, you must stop looking down. It is only scaring you, and we must keep moving. We are nearly there." His encouraging words were barely making it through the thick veil of sweat and pain that Sarah was feeling. Never before had she taken on a challenge like that. Her soft hands were having a difficult time gripping the rope. She said, "I can't. I can't." Her body began to tremble, and her grip began to weaken.

Taurik worked quickly to get to her, rappelling as quickly as the rope and terrain would allow. "Sarah, don't let go. Hold on! Sarah, you can do this!"

Blood from Sarah's hands stained the rope, but she fought against gravity and the fear of falling.

Taurik was not close enough to grab her if she fell. She screamed, and he continued down, passing the bloody spot on the rope. Her scream ended, and he stopped in his tracks. He continued down the face of the rock, and when he crossed the next ledge, Sarah was dangling by her knapsack. Sar caught her only yards from certain death.

Taurik's descent quickened, and he joined the other two at the bottom. He grabbed Sarah, held her tightly, and took her face in his hands. "I thought I lost you."

Sarah's hands were badly cut and burned. Her body was trembling, but she remained collected.

Taurik turned to Sar and said, "I am sorry I doubted you." He bowed to the young lad.

Sar touched Taurik's shoulder. "Hold on to that not, Sir Taurik. Now we go forward together to help Sarah. It is our common destiny."

"We will need fresh water to clean your wounds," Taurik said to Sarah. Looking to the horizon, he continued, "The nearest freshwater stream is far from here, and your wounds need tending before infection sets in."

Sarah was sitting with her legs folded and her hands on her knees. The blood had stopped streaming from the wounds, but the burn was intense. "What about the goblet Binate gave me before we left Gropal?"

"Yes," he said. "That would work. There is a stream not too far from here, but the water is tainted with waste and debris."

Taurik helped Sarah to her feet, and they started off toward the river.

Sarah looked to Sar and asked, "What waste?" Looking between the two, she said, "What kind of debris?" She couldn't help but notice their mutual sadness.

ᴂ Chapter 5

FOR MANY MINUTES, THE TRIO WALKED IN SILENCE.
Sar finally said, "Years ago, there was a mighty war between the clans of my people. Many survived from my clan, but many more did not. The ones who did went into hiding, as I explained before. Although we did not hide our faces, we hid ourselves and our beliefs as best we could. Clan leaders knew there was something different about us, but they could not see it for some reason. The river was the central point of our wars, and many bled there. Debris from evil was left to rot and taint the waters forever. Only the coming of the One could remove the curse my people left on it all those years ago." Sar's eyes wandered to the path in front of him.

Taurik held some branches aside for them as they passed. Slowly but surely, they made their way through the thick brush to the riverside.

Coming out to the river's edge, Sarah saw what Sar had been trying to explain. The day was bright on both sides of the path, but where the river flowed in the middle, it was dark. It was like dusk on a foggy day. It was quiet all around, except where their feet landed. To her left and right, water ran slowly. Sarah saw something sticking out of the water not twenty feet from her and made her way through the murky water to investigate. Neither of her companions stopped her.

Sarah walked through the water and touched the object. Her vision changed, and her surroundings changed along with it. At that moment, she was standing in the middle of a mighty battle. Her hand was resting on the armor of a fallen soldier, and all around, metal clattered and clanged. She heard the screams of the wounded and the battle cries of the victors.

Through the sea of warring Kenjubs, which was the name of Sar's people, Sarah spotted Sar and his father. Nib took off the uniform of a dead soldier and put it around his son. He did the same thing for himself. She saw a few more soldiers doing the same thing when her attention was drawn to the river. It was heavy with bodies and blood, and almost all were wearing the uniform that Sar and Nib had donned. The uniform, from what Sarah could see, was a handsome one, but before she could decipher any more of the horrors of that day, she lost her balance and her grip on the armor.

The vision disappeared, and she came back to Taurik and Sar. Sarah staggered backward until the cold, muddy water was at her waist. She knew what had happened. Having the vision rattled her—but not anywhere near as much as the emotional transference that came along with it.

Taurik leaned in to catch her fall but was only quick enough to get her hand.

Sarah noticed Taurik looking at her blushed cheeks. She said softly, "They had no choice." Looking over to Sar, she added, "You were only a small child at war. You had no choice but to wear the uniform of your enemy. Your father did what was best. I would have done the same. I only saw a few. Was that all that survived?"

She saw the pain on Sar's face and knew only a few survived. The anguish in her heart for Sar was too much, and she began to weep. She took out the goblet from her pack and remembered the wound on her hand. She reached into the water and filled the goblet to its rim. She let the water flow and was astonished to see the wound on her hand becoming clean and fully healed within seconds. Sarah reached down and refilled the goblet. She let the water from the goblet fall down easily into the muddy river. She thought about how dreadful the battle had been and wanted nothing more at that moment than to erase the memory scarred on the land in front of her.

The water from the goblet merged with the water from the river and became as clear as the empathy in her heart. Soon the length of the river was cleared of all of the mud and armor of the Kenjubs that had fallen there.

Taurik stepped back a pace.

Sar bowed to her and said, "Truly you are the one who holds the light we had been fighting for. My people will now rest."

Taurik filled his water pouch, and Sarah filled hers. Before Sarah put the goblet back into her bag, she looked it over and drank from it. Her skin tingled as the water went down. It was pure and delicious.

Sar and Taurik drank from the stream. Pointing to his water pouch, Taurik said, "Sar, you will not go thirsty, my friend."

Sar nodded, smiled, and began his ascent to the other side of the ravine.

Sarah finished packing the goblet, taking care to wrap it even better than before. She looked over her hand again and watched Taurik move toward her. "Did you know I could do that?" she asked.

Taurik looked at her with a wide smile and said, "No. Did you?" He turned to go over to the embankment and looked back at her with a smile.

She joined him at the slope and started to climb giving him a small grin to let him know that she did appreciate his humor.

When they reached the top, Sar was waiting for them. "So far, we have not been noticed here."

Taurik nodded and motioned for them to continue.

That stretch of forest was different than the ones before in look and feel. Sarah could feel the cold in her veins. She could hear the whispers of the shadows and sense the eyes of the Dark Lord on her every step. The chill Sarah felt did not go unnoticed.

From behind her, Taurik began to speak slowly but clearly. He said, "What you are sensing, Lady Sarah, is very real. Do not discount what your instincts are telling you. This stretch of the journey is the most difficult of all. You will be tested in almost every fashion."

Sarah stopped and turned to look at him, but Taurik motioned for her to continue walking. She asked, "Why is it me who keeps getting tested while the two of you seem to get off free?"

Looking up and motioning in a circle around his body, Taurik replied, "He is not interested in us. If this were any other time—and you were any other person—the journey through these parts would be much more for us than it has been thus far. But you are the central focus of the Dark Lord's desire, and we are merely a distraction to him."

They continued walking through the dark forest.

Taurik said, "For you, Lady Sarah, that is why we are so concerned. He will try to get you before we can get you to my father." He stopped, took Sarah's arm, and had her face him. "He will use every trick to get you to stand at his side so that the power you alone possess will be put to evil instead of good."

Sarah released her arm, nodded, and kept walking. She understood what Taurik was saying, but she was also trying to figure something out. A piece of this puzzle was starting to come clear, but instead of providing an answer, it only created another question.

The light was starting to fade, and they had not stopped to eat or rest. Sarah was beginning to grow weary. She bent down on the side of the trail and grabbed a long branch that had fallen from a tall, crooked tree. She made do with it as a walking stick, and Taurik smiled.

Sarah tried to put the pieces together, and when her thoughts finally came full circle, she said, "There is a part of all of this that I just can't figure out."

Taurik looked at her but said nothing. Sar, too, kept his quiet pace. He did look back over his shoulder either.

Sarah said, "There is one thing that I just can't figure out."

Sar said, "What is it, Miss Sarah?"

Sarah glared over her shoulder at Taurik. "I have been told of the man they call Rika, and I've been told that we are headed there. I have also been told that Rika, his kin, and his subjects are dear friends of the people of Gropal. The part I don't get is how two places could be so friendly with such terrible travel between them. I just can't see how those in either place would jeopardize their lives to go have afternoon tea with the other." She ended her thought with a definite note of thick sarcasm. She stopped walking, and with the slightest hint of breathlessness, she said, "I'm not going another step until that is explained to me."

Sar and Taurik looked at each other for a few seconds.

"I knew it!" Sarah turned in a complete circle and said, "There's another way around, isn't there!" Her voice was far from kind or patient as she looked at Sar and Taurik. She walked up to Taurik and looked him square in the eyes. "Isn't there?"

Taurik looked down at her and said, "Yes."

"I can't believe it!" Sarah threw her walking stick to the ground and paced back and forth. "I can't believe I trusted you—and you knowingly put my life on the line time after time. And all along, you knew there was another, much safer way to get to." She snarled and said, "The land of Eslinar."

Taurik said, "Please, Sarah, hear me out."

Sarah would not stop. She navigated around him and grabbed her stick. "I trusted you. I thought you were being up front with me. All along, I thought we had to come this way!"

"We did!" Taurik raised his voice to her for the first time. "Listen to me!" He grabbed her arms, almost hurting her.

Sar stepped in and said, "Miss Sarah, we had no choice. Listen to him." His voice calmed both of them down. He walked around the perimeter and looked out for attackers. "We can't stay here long."

Taurik said, "This was the only path that would have been enough for all of us, including you, to determine and embrace your strengths and weaknesses." Pausing for a second, he turned away. "If we had taken the traveled road, you would never have encountered what you did back at the river. That, Sarah, is only one example of why we took this path."

Sarah nodded and said, "Am I to understand then that the only way you and your people would know if I was the *one* you speak of is if I didn't die trying to get to Rika." She waited for an answer.

"I regret that is the truth of it," Sar said.

Taurik said, "I didn't look at it that way until now."

Sarah saw the anguish in Taurik's eyes and calmed down. "Well, we can't stay here for much longer. You said it yourself, didn't you? Lead on, Sar."

With that, the trio was on its way again.

Sar picked up his pace a bit. Sarah looked back at Taurik and gave him one of her best smiles. She knew in her heart that Taurik was no liar and had no ill will for her.

Sarah was unaware that he was undoubtedly falling in love with her but could not say it at that time. Not to her, not to anyone.

They moved fast, and the terrain was hard. Sarah was getting used to the conditions of her journey and needed less sleep than before. She also needed less food and drink, and therefore, she needed to stop less often to relieve herself. Sarah felt strong and sure-footed. Soon enough, she would learn that the powers of that world were changing her. The essence of her very being was growing.

In Taurik's training, he was warned that if she was the one they had waited for, her strengths would come out fast, but as fast as the good would come, he was also taught, the evil she would need to fight would follow.

Sar had said very little in the hours after Sarah's outburst. He was paying close attention to the path. Between watching for attackers and plotting their route, his mind drifted to the miracle he had witnessed at the river. He had waited a lifetime, and others even longer, for her to come. The others had sacrificed their lives for what she could return to them. To know that her fate was not in his hands was tearing at him from the deepest part of his soul. His people, what was left of them, needed her to succeed. If she did not, all the good his people had fought for would be lost forever.

Taurik had similar thoughts. He tried not to think of such an ending since that would mean that Sarah had fallen into darkness. In doing so, she would either meet her demise or oversee the demise of all that was good. Neither scenario struck him as pleasant. He hoped she would be able to trust them, even knowing they had hidden part of the truth from her. He prayed she understood what they had to do. There had been many councils prior to her arrival on the proper way to proceed, and the many judges had made their decisions.

Sarah asked, "Will we be camping soon? It's getting dark."

Taurik said, "We can stop at the top." He pointed to the top of the hill they were climbing. "From that vantage point, we should be able to see any dangers before they reach us."

Sar said, "I agree. The peak is good."

Sarah nodded and continued to follow Sar. Between ducking under branches and holding aside tree limbs, she put together a plan in her head for how to get out from under the guard of Taurik and Sar. Even if they had meant no harm, they had created one of the hardest wounds to heal: lost trust.

When the trio reached the top, Taurik and Sar checked the surroundings before putting down their things. When they decided it was safe, they started to gather wood for a fire. Sarah would have helped, but her mind was preoccupied with her plan. She was slowly convincing herself that leaving was the best thing for her to do.

The three of them sat around the small fire Sar built and shared again from Tinbe's pot. With full stomachs, they sat back and got as comfortable as they could.

As he propped himself up against a large tree, Taurik said, "I will stay awake. You two get some rest."

Sar said, "Only for a short while—then I will stay watch. You need to rest too. Yes?"

Taurik watched Sarah set herself up against a tree a few yards from the fire. She was still close enough that the warmth comforted her. He watched her looking into the fire. She was far away in thought. The last week of her life had been anything but normal or expected. If their roles had been reversed, he was uncertain if he would have had enough strength or grace to get as far as she had.

He watched as her beautiful eyes started to flutter with

fatigue and finally give way to it. His heart was heavy with worry. Sarah's journey was not yet half over, and they were not going at the pace they needed to be. The more he thought about what to do next, the more drained he became. He saw no resolution except to continue on the path as planned. Taurik's eyes batted as he threw his head back, trying to jolt some energy into them. Before he knew it, he had fallen into a much-needed sleep.

As the moon filled the sky and the stars sang out their names, the three of them slept. Unprotected by Sar and Taurik's senses, Sarah began to dream.

Her eyes fluttered underneath their protective shields. Her eyes opened, and she looked over to Sar and Taurik. They were both sleeping soundly. Sarah got up slowly and packed her bag, but she did not zipper it. She did not want to risk waking them. She did not know where she was to go, but she knew her destiny would only be fulfilled if she left them behind.

The idea of walkabout came back to Sarah for a moment, but she quickly pushed the thought from her mind. The memory of home was becoming too painful, mainly the sadness of her mother when she didn't return. With her bag all set, she turned from the burning embers and stepped into the forest, continuing on their course. Before the camp was out of sight, she looked back and saw Taurik. He looked so peaceful. Sarah hoped her quest would lead her to him again.

Twenty minutes later, Sar awoke. He stretched a bit and stared at the red embers. When he saw that Taurik was sleeping, his heart began to race. He quickly stood and saw that Sarah and all of her belongings were gone. "No!" Sar dashed over to Taurik and lifted him to his feet by his collar. As soon as he got him to a standing position, a hard blow came to his midsection. Down he went, gasping for air.

"What the hell is the matter with you?" Taurik swiftly moved away and grabbed the nearest branch as a weapon.

Sar could only point to the area where Sarah had been and whispered, "She's gone." He put his head down for a second and started to stand with the help of tree.

Taurik followed Sar's finger with his eyes but did not lighten his stance until he saw what Sar was pointing at. He quickly went over to Sarah's resting spot and looked around frantically for tracks. Turning in one direction and then taking steps in the other, he looked into the surrounding forest. There was no sign of her. He wanted to yell for her but knew it would only draw attention to them. They could do no good—or worse—if captured.

Running out of places to look, Taurik sat down in front of the embers. "I hadn't needed rest when we arrived here. How could I have fallen that deep asleep and not heard her leave?" He took out his knife and began to carve the end of the stick he had grabbed moments earlier.

Sar was still holding himself as he sat down where Taurik had been. "Much of his magic is here. I can feel it. It is possible that you were not responsible for your sleep."

Taurik nodded and continued to carve the branch.

Sar stood and said, "We should go. We need to find her. She cannot fall into his hands."

Taurik stopped what he was doing and looked up to Sar. "And which way would you have us go? We have no way of knowing her direction. I am familiar with surviving in the woods, but I am not a tracker. To wander aimlessly in search of her would only prove futile for all of us. We will not be of any use to her at all if we are killed. We will stay here till morning—and then we will continue on the road to Eslinar. There my father will give us counsel."

Sar said, "So it is lost then? She will not survive a night out here on her own." He looked deeper into the embers that were growing back into flames as Taurik stirred them and added timber.

Taurik said, "She is stronger and more resilient than either of us might think." He sat back. "She has showed nothing but strength and trust since the moment I met her. Her fear only comes through on occasion, but the trust in herself is growing with every minute. She has already grown more confident, and she is now aware of some of her abilities. She will no doubt put some of them to the test." He stopped for a minute and looked over to Sar with sad eyes. "I have no doubt she will be tested. I just hope that our dishonesty didn't decide the outcome."

Sar nodded and soon fell asleep.

ᘓ Chapter 6

Aᴼᴼ FTER WALKING THROUGH THE THICK BRUSH FOR A LONG
while, Sarah began to get worn out. The rest she had
gotten earlier was not good enough, and although she was
stronger than ever before, rest was needed. The pressure
dissipated, and a calm came over her as she looked for a
place to stop.

Coming to an open patch where the undergrowth
seemed to have been pressed down in a circular shape,
Sarah dropped her bag against a tree. She knew better
than to continue during the night, but before getting
comfortable, she looked all around to see if anything was
waiting to attack.

After many minutes of straining her eyes to see through
shadows, Sarah decided it was safe to sit and let her body
relax. She sat back and stared through a hole in the trees
to the endless stars. Her fatigue quickly took over, and she
soon fell asleep. There were no dreams; there was nothing
but deep rest until morning.

Sarah awoke to the beautiful sound of a bird singing.
She opened her eyes and looked around, still feeling a bit
paranoid. Sarah didn't see anything or anyone, and she

stood up and stretched. The ground had been her bed for days, and her bones missed the comfort of Vente's cottage. When she heard the beautiful sound, she grabbed her bag, straightened her dress, and followed it. She was quite hungry but decided to stop later. She was only interested in finding the creature that was making the alluring sound.

When first she heard it, it was straight ahead, but after few minutes, she heard it to her left a bit. She adjusted her path and caught a glimpse of the creature's tail. It was gorgeous with colors she had only seen in paintings. She couldn't tell much from that quick look, but the view was enough to keep her moving toward it.

When Sarah remembered she was still in the land of the Dark Lord, she stopped dead in her tracks. She feared that following the creature was a trap. Sarah felt small and lost until she remembered that she could not truly be lost without an intended destination. With that thought, she felt much better about things.

As Sarah continued to walk, she started to really look at her surroundings. She noticed how all the greens and browns—and even the colors of the flowers she passed—were all subtly muffled in a grayish fog. The fog was not thick, but it was enough to limit visibility to about thirty yards.

Slowly, the landscape was turning from forest to rock. She noticed a jumble of rocks appearing where dirt had been a moment before. A few times, an unexpected rock disturbed her footing. Sarah continued on her way until she was drained by hunger and thirst.

She found a small brook that was void of any dangers. She set her things down at the side of the stream, got out her goblet, and drank from it with full gulps. The water rejuvenated Sarah enough for her to carefully pick out the driest limbs from the surrounding trees and make a small fire. She had some stew from her pot; she was growing accustomed to the taste and found comfort in it.

The night came slowly, and there was little difference in the ambience. It was darker, but the fog remained. The sound of water running was soothing enough that she began to relax.

Sarah tried to fall asleep, but she remembered the fright in Taurik and Sar's eyes. She could not relax enough to fall asleep completely. As the sun rose, she began to realize that Taurik and the others meant her no harm, but she still felt betrayed.

The sounds began to change. One sound overlapped another; soon all she could hear was the water. The noise drowned everything else out. It grew louder and louder by the second. Sarah opened her eyes in time to see a wall of water coming at her from upstream. She grabbed her bag just before the water knocked her over.

Surrounded by cold, blue water, the white foam from the thrashing waves tried to hold Sarah down. Her eyes opened instinctively as she tried to find the surface. She surfaced long enough to get a gulp of air and was forced down again by one of the many spiraling arms. She finally was able to get her bearings enough to keep her head in the air.

She was fully aware of her predicament and knew she needed to get out of there quickly. Sarah feared for her life. The water churned violently, but she was able to gain control over her body while avoiding being slammed against the boulders that littered the water's path.

She saw a branch from a fallen tree in front of her and knew it was her only chance. Only a dozen yards past the limb, the water plummeted to the earth below. She swam as hard as she could to align herself with it and let the rushing water do the rest.

When the branch got very close, Sarah realized how fast the water was moving. By then, it was too late. She was slammed into it with such a force that the wind was knocked from her lungs. Her bag caught its edge, and Sarah held it long enough to grab around its girth with her cold, wet hands.

She kept her eyes closed as her body swung to and fro. When she opened her eyes, the sight made her grip the branch tighter—and thinking about what would happen if she let go or if the branch broke made her cling to it even tighter.

Don't look down. That's what they say, right? Her eyes wandered past her toes and down to the valley below. She could not tell just how high she was, but things down below looked quite small.

She caught her breath, opened her eyes, looked around, and thought, *I can't stay here.* She started to shimmy her way up and across the branch.

She got close enough to the edge that a jagged rock sticking just slightly out from the wall served as a small foothold. Sarah wedged her foot in, pushed with her leg, and pulled with her arms. She quickly put the other leg around the top of the branch. Keeping her momentum, she stood and took two very wobbly steps to dry land.

She fell to the ground, gasping for air.

A deep voice said, "That was some stunt."

She jumped up, ready to fight, but swung herself up so hard that she started to stagger backward. Sarah had not made it that far away from the cliff when she landed. She tried not to fall off the edge, staggering forward and back and to the side. She tried to catch herself, but she knew she was falling—and her heart screamed death.

A strong hand grabbed her wrist, walked her a few feet away from the cliff, and sat her against a slightly angled tree.

It took her a minute to focus on the man who had saved her, but when she did, she was happily surprised that he did not look dangerous. She met his bright green eyes with a half-smile. She stood up and brushed twigs from her drenched clothes. "You scared me half to death! Do you always sneak up on people like that, scaring them so much that they nearly fall and you *have* to save them?"

The man smiled and put her bag on his shoulder. With a slight tug to guide her in his direction, he said, "I didn't have to."

With that, Sarah began traveling with a new companion. Sarah had grown accustomed to following the guides who were put in her path. It seemed as though she was much better off when she did. The land was new to her and filled with things, people, and creatures she was unaccustomed to. She felt it was much safer to follow a stranger than to wander aimlessly alone. With those thoughts, she quietly let the handsome man carry her bag for a little while—until she remembered the goblet, the pan, and all of the other contents. She wondered how much of it had survived the flash flood. She did not think her clothes and other travel items had fared very well.

Sarah caught up to him and grabbed lightly at the bag. She felt the tension in his arm when she did and pulled a little harder until he let go. "Who are you?" Sarah asked, still following the muscular man.

"Who I am is of no matter," he said over his shoulder. "What does matter is that we get back to my quarters to get you some dry clothes before you catch your death."

"I have been told that darkness is in these parts. How do I know that you won't hurt me when we get there?"

"You don't." The man kept walking and didn't even look back to see if Sarah was following.

Before long, they came upon a wooden hut with a wicker roof. The door was jagged and falling off its hinges, but the man opened it with ease.

They both entered, and Sarah was pleased that the inside was a lot cozier than it looked from the outside. There was a bed in the far corner and table set with three chairs. There was a long counter to the right on which sat a teakettle, pots with many types of herbs, and a number of large knives.

Choking back a rush of fear, Sarah pointed to the large knives and asked, "What are those for?"

"Food isn't prepared for us here, Miss. We hunt for what we eat." He came out of the far closet and handed her a towel.

Sarah asked, "What is your name? The least you can do is tell me that."

The man turned and walked slowly over to her. Putting his hands on her arms, he said softly, "I don't think you would believe me if I told you my name. Besides, I am not known by my name—only by my title." His eyes filled with sadness as he walked over to a small chair in the corner. His wavy hair hid his face for a moment, but with a handsome gesture, he moved it away and met Sarah's focused gaze. Gesturing for her to take a seat on the other small chair, he said, "Please sit."

"Okay." Sarah made her way past the nook in the kitchen, walked over the round braided rug, and took a seat on the wooden chair. She did not want to get too comfortable. Her clothes were still soaked, and she didn't like how it felt.

Sarah's frustration was building. Everyone around her knew what was happening, but she was always in the dark. She was a bit flustered that she had followed this nameless stranger who—like everyone else—was telling her nothing.

As she sat, the man went to the kitchen and poured two glasses of liquid. He walked to her and held out the glass, looking at her intently.

Sarah noticed his gaze and returned it carefully as she took the glass from his hand. She sniffed the liquid and slowly took a small mouthful. Sarah knew that taste. It was very much like the brew she enjoyed on the morning of her departure. She sat back in the chair and took a deep breath. Her body relaxed more than it had in days. She was enjoying her brew so much that she momentarily forgot the man was still there. When she looked up over the rim of her cup, he was sitting across the room and sipping his cup in the same manner.

He said, "Feel better?"

Sarah said, "Yes, much. Thank you."

Sarah started to shift in her seat, but she took another sip of the brew and again was comforted.

"Did you get hurt in the rapids?" he asked.

"Physically no, but I think my pride took a beating," Sarah said.

The man looked impressed. "You are stronger than I had thought."

"As you had thought?"

The man stood up and started over to the sink with his cup. "I meant no harm by that. I'm just quite impressed with your strength."

Even though Sarah didn't know this man—or have any reason to trust him—she couldn't help but feel a rush run through her body. "Well, I am happy for you then. I'm glad I did whatever it is that I did," Sarah said with a wry smile and a twinkle in her eye.

"So, stranger, what's your name? Or is it a secret?"

The man faced her and said, "You might not stay if I tell you who I am." Returning her wry smile, he continued, "And I do so enjoy your company."

Sarah was impressed by the strong man's sense of humor. That was a hard combination to find back home.

"You haven't been anything but helpful. Why would I leave because of your name?" As she spoke, the answer came to her. She sat back in her chair and looked the man over. From head to toe, she could not see what was so scary about this man that he could have been given such a terrible title. Upon further examination of the Dark Lord, she could see he knew she had figured out his title. Before she could think of anything else, she blurted out, "So why the Dark Lord? What is so dark about you that people fear?" She figured they had been quite candid with each other— why stop now? She sat up in her chair, put her cup onto the floor, clasped her hands, and looked at him. She waited for his answer, not caring about her wet clothes.

He walked to the counter and poured water into the kettle. As he turned on the flame to make tea, he looked up and said, "My name is Arron. The title of Dark Lord came to me by no measure of my own. I am ruler here, but my biggest fault is the lack of law. There are few of them, but the ones that are in place, I do punish dearly for breaking."

In little more than a minute, all that Sarah had been told and believed to be true was in doubt again. *Could this man truly have been so evil?* Her mind was too tired to figure out the maze.

"Are we resting here tonight?" she asked.

The look of genuine surprise that Sarah didn't run out of there screaming was written all over Arron's face.

He said, "We will rest here tonight if you desire. Tomorrow at dawn, we eat—and then will go to my home."

Sarah said, "This isn't your home?"

Arron chuckled softly. "No." He motioned for her to join him and led her down a small hallway lit only by the candle in his hand. At the end, Arron opened a door to a cozy room with a bed and a nightstand. There was little else in the room, but Sarah knew she would be asleep in no time. The accommodations were not a source of worry.

"I hope this will do for you," Arron said as he turned to leave.

Sarah felt a rush come over her and turned quickly to him. "Thank you." She was shocked that they were looking straight into each other's eyes.

Arron nodded, handed Sarah the candle, and backed away into the darkness of the hallway.

Sarah closed the door and took a breath. She was utterly confused by the stories she had heard. She felt no wrong in Arron, and with that comforting thought, she changed into dry clothes and fell asleep.

Sarah awoke to the smell of bacon. She got up from the bed with vigor, straightened the blankets, pulled back her hair, and noticed that her clothes had dried. She took in a deep breath of fresh air from the open windows on the far side of the room.

Walking for the door, Sarah suddenly remembered who was cooking out there. She thought briefly about everything she had been warned about and compared it to her own experience with him. In a moment, she came to her own conclusion. *They're crazy.* She opened the bedroom door and walked out to eat with Arron.

In the Dark Lord, Sarah couldn't see all the horrors she had been told—and even worse things that were implied. Arron was just a man as far as she could see, and she did not fear him. He turned from the spitting bacon and smiled. "Well, good morning to you. Sleep well?"

"Yes. Thanks." Sarah was famished.

"Please sit." Arron pointed to a table with two simple plates and saucers.

Sarah sat down, and as soon as she opened her napkin, Arron delivered the hot meal. She was impressed. He had timed it so well. She only spent a moment on that thought because the food was warm and so good. Nothing else crossed her mind for the next few minutes.

Arron sat down with his plate and took a few bites. The sun highlighted Sarah's hair and the contours of her neck. When she looked up, her blue eyes were so beautiful that

Arron felt a warmth come over him that he had not felt in a long time—and it had nothing to do with the food. "Would you willingly come with me to my home?"

Sarah finished chewing and took a sip of her drink. Her mind was saying that it was not the best idea she had ever had, but the rest of her was screaming otherwise. "I'm not sure. Where would we go? I definitely need a guide here, but I have been warned about you."

"Oh yes, the Dark Lord thing," he said with a sigh.

"Yes. I don't get how you could be so blasé about that. The things I have been told were not very flattering—to say the least. But since I've met you, you have saved me from certain death, took me in, fed me, and let me sleep. I just don't see any reason why I can't go with you." She took another bite, smirking as she looked at him.

"I think we are going to get along very well." Arron stood and took his dishes to the washing area. He turned back toward her and grabbed his jacket. "We will leave in two hours. Make yourself at home until then. I'll be back to get you." He closed the door behind him.

Sarah didn't know what to make of Arron. She was having a hard time putting together what Taurik and the others were warning her about and the hospitality she had been shown. The two ideas did not match. She finished her food, put her dishes in the sink, and ran water over them. Her mind flooded with memories of her mother teaching her that water was a cook's best friend.

Looking around the cabin, she took it all in for the first time. The small chairs and the fireplace reminded her of home. The kitchen table was set up right in front of the window. As a child, she would eat breakfast and watch the falling snow, hoping she wouldn't have to go to school that day.

She started to think of her career. She couldn't find anything in her that missed the hustle and bustle that photojournalism created. Even after everything she had been through, the idea of it all still stressed her out. She shook her head and wandered back into the bedroom. She put her meager belongings into her sack and saw her journal. She took it out, went over to the small table, and began to write.

> Hi there,
>
> So far, this journey has been riddled with the unthinkable. I still have a hard time believing that it's all real, but there is a fear growing inside me that my entrance into this place might be irreversible. I am also a bit confused about the warnings Taurik, Sar, and Tinbe gave me about the Dark Lord. I met him, and I don't see the horrors they told me about. He seems kind enough. He saved my life from the rapids. He took me in from the night and fed me. He let me sleep in his cabin, and he made me a wonderful breakfast.
>
> He asked if I would go with him to his home. I was a little hesitant, but in light of the way he has personally made me feel thus far, I am inclined to go.
>
> Did I mention that he is very handsome? I can't believe I am saying that.

Here I am trapped in a parallel world, and I am thinking this man is cute. God, is there something wrong with me?

I miss my mother. I hope she's not too worried. How awful this must be for her. Right now, I have no way back. Just forward.

She closed her journal, brushed her teeth, and finished packing. Arron had not returned yet, but Sarah put her bag on her back and closed the door behind her.

❧ Chapter 7

WHILE SHE WAITED, SHE LOOKED AROUND THE CABIN. IT WAS not a bad size to be out there in the middle of nowhere. The wood was worn in spots and weathered quite nicely in others. The trees surrounding it were full of autumn leaves. This was a little puzzling to her due to the warmth of the air and breeze. There was a bench not too far from where she was standing, and as she walked over to it, she could see that it was in front of a fire pit. She sat down and took in the scenery.

It was very quiet except for the sound of the leaves in the wind and the occasional bird singing. She started to daydream about the possibilities of the day and found herself thinking of Arron.

A snap came from the woods behind her.

She swung around and was stunned to see Tinbe. She stood and started toward him. "Tinbe! What are you doing here?" she said with a smile.

"Follow you, I have been. Since you left." He nodded, grabbed her hand, and started to lead her away from the cabin.

"What are you doing?" Sarah said as she struggled to get her hand free.

Tinbe looked up at her, loosened his grip, and said, "You are being led astray, young Sarah. I wasn't to interfere with your journey, but stand by and see, I cannot." He shook his head, and a sorrow-filled expression passed over his worn face.

Sarah looked at him, and her face went cold. "You've been following me the whole time!" Taking a few steps back, she continued, "You saw the flood? You saw him save me? Why would you still say I'm being led astray?" She took a couple deep breaths, walked over to Tinbe, and said, "You have been so sweet to me, Tinbe. I don't mean to shout at you. I don't see what you see. I don't feel what you feel. I was welcomed into your home and was given shelter and food—but barely any truth. I come out here on my own, and this man saved my life. He took me in and gave me a place to sleep—just like you—but he gave me the truth, which you did not. Not even when I asked for it."

Tinbe looked up at her and said, "Miss Sarah, I hope only to see safely to the end you come."

Sarah softened a bit and knelt down in front of Tinbe. "I know you care. I can tell you do. But all of you have said it so many times that this is my journey, and this is the way I want to go. I must see for myself. I feel different than I did when I got here. I know I can handle this."

Tinbe's eyes widened. "Ah, your strength grows, it does. Your powers are many. So young they are though, and so you are new to them."

Sarah was puzzled. She only meant that she felt better than she had. She felt more confident and stronger than when she arrived. She was about to ask Tinbe what powers he was talking about when she heard footsteps in the woods to the side of the cabin.

Tinbe grabbed her arm and said, "Careful, Miss Sarah. Stay with you, I will."

Sarah turned to see who was coming, and when she turned back, Tinbe was gone.

Arron said, "So, it's official—you are coming. I am pleased." He looked a little ruffled and motioned for Sarah to wait while he entered the cabin.

When he came out a few minutes later, Sarah had regained her composure. "Are we going to your home now?" she asked.

"Yes. Yes, we are." He met her stride, took her hand, and his eyes met hers. "I am glad you are coming, Sarah." He placed a soft kiss on her forehead, smiled, and motioned for Sarah to follow.

Sarah could pay attention to where she was going only in the moments she was not in awe of the beauty of the countryside. She was baffled that it appeared to be completely void of the horrors and darkness she had been warned about. She said, "This land is nothing like I had heard."

Arron chuckled and said, "This land is what the observer desires to see." He stopped walking and turned to her. "What do you desire to see, Sarah?"

Sarah was taken aback by the directness of his question. "I don't know."

Arron turned with the smile Sarah was starting to like quite a bit and said, "Up ahead, you must watch yourself. It can get quite slippery."

A few hundred feet later, they came to the top of a magnificent waterfall. It was stunning to look at, but when Arron started to stride across the top of it, she saw that it was quite a rocky drop to the bottom. A little shaky but not thrown, Sarah started out behind Arron and stepped where he stepped.

Arron reached the other side and leaned against a colorful tree.

For a moment, Sarah felt very confident—and the height was of no concern. Her feet took on a stride of their own. She stopped in the middle of the falls, looked up to Arron, and smiled. She started again, and her ankle twisted on a pebble. She only lost her footing enough to have to reach down, but when her hand touched the rock beneath her feet, the world around her changed. The beautiful trees turned dark and barren, and the sky hazed over with a dark cloud. She heard screaming in the winds that blew around her like a weak cyclone, and the whispers of children put chills up her spine.

She stood up, released her fingers from the rock, and looked at Arron with fear-filled eyes.

He was still smiling, and as fast as the vision came on, it disappeared. The trees returned to their beautiful colors, the water calmed, the sky cleared. Within moments, Sarah's heart rate returned to normal. She continued over the rocks and reached the other side.

Arron took her hand and kissed it. "That was, I believe, the best thing I have seen in a long time." He turned away and continued on.

Sarah followed him, staying quite close. She was flabbergasted, but she could not bring herself to say anything—even though she felt more comforted around

Arron than she had near anyone thus far. He apparently hadn't noticed, and something told her it was not for sharing. She just knew it.

With Tinbe's warning in the front of her mind, she continued on. The sound of the breeze in the leaves soothed her. For a moment, she became one with her thoughts. When they came to the top of a steep incline, she saw the Dark Lord's castle. Sarah looked over, and Arron was looking at her. *Probably to see my reaction*, she thought. She was mindful of her facial expressions as she looked out over the land. A massive gray building stood in the middle of a vast prairie of grain and plowed earth. Her mouth fell open, and she closed it quickly. She smiled sheepishly and followed Arron down the rocks on the face of the canyon.

Arron noticed that Sarah was no longer using her hands to steady herself. He knew her powers were getting stronger. He wondered if she knew. He hoped that she did not—at least not yet. Arron motioned for Sarah to go ahead of him. He took great pleasure in watching her. He thought she was beautiful, and he hoped she would accept him when the time came.

At the bottom of the rocks, Sarah looked across the vast field. She was awed by the size of the castle. "This is yours?" she asked. She didn't think such a gentle man would reside in a place that seemed so impersonal and cold.

He smiled and said, "Yes. It has been in my family for many generations. It is large and drafty at times, but it serves its purpose quite well."

"Its purpose?" Sarah asked. "What purpose is that, may I ask?"

Arron stopped walking and thought for a moment. "The purpose is quite difficult to explain, Miss Sarah." He pointed to the people in the field. "Those over there are the harvesters of our grain, and those over there are the packers of that grain. Everyone has a purpose here—a duty if you will—and as one does, the many will do."

"Sounds like a riddle to me." Sarah still didn't know enough. She took his answer as it was, and they continued toward the main gate. One part of what Arron had said kept creeping into her thoughts: *As one does, the many will do.* She turned around when they reached the gate, and many more people were working. She noticed the similarity of their clothing, but she could not make out their faces.

The castle gates opened, and many loud cranks and levers sounded as if they were put together with hundred-year-old chains. Sarah remembered a lesson that her mother had tried to teach her many years ago: "Don't jump in if you are unsure how to get out." Sarah realized that she had not done anything to answer that very important question. How would she get out if she wanted to? She thought back to her surveillance of the front walls and did not recall any other doors. The front gate was not an easy escape if she decided to leave. It would take at least two other men to operate the gate's levers, and that was not to mention the sound of it opening. It sure would not be quiet.

There was no answer she could think of at that point,

and she had come all that way already. She decided to bury those fears for the time being. Arron had made her feel wonderful back at the cabin and during the journey to the castle. She was comforted to know he was there, and within a few minutes, the fears she had were all but gone.

Inside the gate, people were carrying bundles and working on things. They walked past the stables, and she made a note of where it was since she loved horses. She glanced in as they walked by and saw a number of fine-looking animals.

Arron kept walking, and she continued to follow him. Everyone in the city looked down as they passed. She couldn't tell if they were afraid. She had read stories in her childhood about how it was an insult to look into the eyes of some kings. *Is that what it is like here?* She noticed that not one person in the courtyard stopped or looked at them. Not one person seemed at all curious about who she was.

She caught the eye of a small child in a brown linen dress on top of a barrel. The girl's parents were cleaning up some hay a few yards away. There was a fine layer of dirt on her cheeks, and her eyes were a beautiful shade of blue. Time slowed down for a moment, and their eyes met. In that child's eyes, Sarah saw wonder, fear, and gentleness.

The moment ended when the child's mother swooped her up and brought her inside.

Arron said, "Come with me, Sarah." He took her hand with a gentle grip and led her into the main estate.

It was just as overwhelming as the rest of the grounds, but inside the walls, fine decorations hung in perfect symmetry. Wall candles surrounded tall mirrors and large paintings.

Arron led her up a flight of stairs and down another long corridor. He stopped at a door with an iron flower hanging above it. "I hope it is to your liking." He opened it and allowed Sarah to enter.

She couldn't believe her eyes. She scanned the room briefly before she looked back at Arron. He was smiling at her, enjoying her reaction. Sarah looked back into the room and entered it. The walls were made of carved stone, like some of the old fireplaces she remembered from her home as a kid. Dark green vines grew horizontally across the wall. Candles illuminated the entire room with splendor. A dresser that doubled as a vanity sat against the far right wall, and to her left, fine silk covered a large bed. Far ahead, a large window filled half the wall. It was draped with fabric like the kind in Gropal. She looked out the window and said, "It's stunning."

Night had fallen on the land, and the moon illuminated the sky so brilliantly that the stars were hidden from view. Sarah could see all the surrounding land they had traveled. The streets of the city were coming to life, and a man lit lanterns with a torch. People were coming and going from the taverns, and carriages picked up and delivered goods to stores and people to their destinations.

"I'm glad you approve." Arron joined her at the window. He stood very close to her, and she felt his breath on her neck.

Sarah was distracted when he reached over and pressed part of the wall. The window opened, and the wall separated. He took her hand and led her out onto the balcony. The warm air was accompanied by a gentle breeze.

Arron softly put his hand to her head. He released her hair from the tie she had put it in. The breeze caught her hair, and it blew about. Arron brushed it away from Sarah's face, caressed her cheek, and looked into her eyes. "You are beautiful."

Sarah was overwhelmed with emotion and could say nothing. She touched his hand on her face and closed her eyes.

A voice from the doorway said, "Sire, may I have a word?"

Looking at the man in armor at the door and then back to Sarah, Arron said, "Please make yourself at home. I will return for you. Until then." He kissed her hand and left, closing the door behind him.

Sarah stood on the balcony, surprised by how quickly he had left. She thought for a moment about what it would have been like if he had actually kissed her. She was surprised by how much she had wanted him to.

Her attention returned to the scene below. The lanterns were all lit. The moon had retreated behind a single cloud, unveiling a sky with more stars than Sarah had ever witnessed. People moved about on wagons, and lights flowed out onto the streets from saloons that were operating at full capacity.

She could make out only a small amount of sound from where she stood, but as her eyes scanned the rest of the happenings, she caught the gaze of the little girl. Just as before, the girl's eyes were unwavering. Sarah smiled and waved. Just as the young girl's mother again removed her from where she sat, the girl returned the gesture.

Sarah made a mental note to meet the little girl before

she left, but she felt as though she knew her already. *Who is she?*

Sarah felt the fatigue of the day, and the bed looked more than inviting. After washing up a bit, she sat on it. She was very impressed. The mattress was made of material that could have come straight from the clouds, and the comforter was a thick satin weave. She got into the bed, and after a deep breath and a bit of reflection, she thought of her journal. She was so comfortable that a deep sleep fell over her before she was able to write down the day's events.

The next morning, she was awakened by a loud knock on the door and a woman walking in. "Oh, dear, it is morning. Time to get up to meet the day." The woman put a tray on the table and went over to Sarah. She waited at the side of the bed, moving around its edges to straighten the fabric.

Sarah was not sure, in her half-conscious state, if she approved of that. As a guest, she figured it best to go along with their customs. Her mother had taught her well. With that memory, she pulled the covers off her eyes and tried to focus on the woman.

When the woman came into view, her looks did not match her voice. She was an older woman with hair neatly tied in a bun at the top of her head, and her dress was brilliant purple and gold. Her golden apron was wrapped around her waist and draped around her upper torso, hanging elegantly over her shoulders and spiraling down her back to the floor.

"Lord Arron awaits you for breakfast, miss," she said.

Sitting up, Sarah looked at the woman and asked, "May I ask if this is how everyone starts their morning here?"

"My name is Madam Marilye, and to answer your question, it only starts this way here for those who do not get up." She flipped the covers off Sarah, right down to her feet, and brought over the tray she had carried in.

"What is that?" Sarah asked as she rubbed her eyes.

"That, my dear, is yours for you to wash. You can't very well go to breakfast like that." After a small pause, she looked at Sarah and said, "Can you?"

Taking the linen off the little table, Sarah replied, "I suppose not." She grinned at Marilye for effect.

Sarah sat up, rinsed off her face with one of the cloths, and dried her face and hands with a second cloth. She continued to bathe her body in that manner, feeling very uncomfortable with the lack of privacy.

Madam Marilye went over to a wardrobe at the far corner of the room, took out a long gown, and gave it to Sarah.

Sarah stood in the center of the room on a soft fur carpet. "What is this?" she asked as she caressed the silk.

"This is for you, my dear." Marilye started to take Sarah's measurements. "And it looks as though you are saving me a lot of work. It's just your size."

Sarah thought it was odd. Nothing was ever her size. Sarah was the perfect example of average back home, but that was why she could never find anything that fit. The racks at the local stores were always filled with sizes that were too small or too large for her. The dress fit her perfectly. As it slid over her head, she could feel it forming to her shape—or was her shape forming to it? She was not sure.

Marilye zipped Sarah up gently and turned her around

so she could see how she looked. Through a full-length antique mirror, she saw the black-and-silver dress. It was gorgeous. She was gorgeous. She smiled—and so did Madam Marilye.

After a few moments, Marilye said, "Well, now, aren't you just the pretty thing? Come on. Breakfast is waiting."

"Wait!" Sarah exclaimed. "My knapsack. Where is it?"

"Your what?" Marilye asked.

"My bag. I had it last night when I came in here. I don't see it. Where is it?" She looked around the room frantically.

"Oh, my dear, that thing? I put it in the wardrobe right over there. It was such a ghastly thing. I thought out of sight was best."

Sarah walked quickly to the wardrobe and saw the knapsack on the bottom shelf. "Is it safe here?"

"Safer here than on the floor, I would imagine." Marilye motioned to the door.

Sarah nodded, took one more spin in the mirror, and walked out on the heels of Marilye. Marilye walked rather fast for a woman of her stature and age, but Sarah kept up without issue.

As they walked through the cobblestone halls, Sarah started to look around. There was hustle and bustle inside almost every room they passed, and there was more artwork everywhere. Sculptures, statues, paintings, and murals adorned every wall. She saw much more than the night before and made a mental note to look at them closer when she had a little time. After a few rights and lefts that Sarah tried to commit to memory, they entered a large room.

Madam Marilye stopped suddenly, and Sarah almost

walked right into her, missing by an inch. Looking closer at the scene, she saw that the large table was not set—and no one was sitting at it.

Arron stood in front of the burning fireplace. He motioned to her to sit at a smaller table set for two. Marilye and Sarah exchanged a smile, and then Madam Marilye turned and left, closing the large wooden doors behind her.

Walking over to him, Sarah couldn't help but notice that Arron looked even better after a bath. His outfit made him look much more noble than he had the previous day. His hair was tied back, which stunned Sarah. Now there was no distraction from his gaze.

As he held the chair for her, Arron said, "May I say that you look even more beautiful than I could have imagined?"

Sarah let out a little small giggle. "You imagined?"

Arron sat in his chair and said, "Yes, I have … for some time now."

"How is it that you would have been imagining me—here, in this dress—when I am here by mistake?"

"A mistake, Sarah?" Arron said with a shake of his head and a laugh. "Make no mistake. You being here is no mistake."

"Would you care to explain?" Sarah hardly thought he would actually answer her.

Arron sat back in his seat and looked at Sarah seriously. His beautiful eyes captured her attention, which was becoming a habit.

"I will admit, my lady, that I am a bit surprised you have not been told even a bit about the history of this place or why you have come across it."

Sarah was hesitant to give away how little she really

knew. "I only know what I have been told, which has not been much. I can assure you it has not explained some of the things I've seen."

"I suppose the beginning would be a perfect place to start," Arron said with twinkling eyes. He took a sip of his morning drink and motioned for Sarah to do the same.

Although she was curious about Arron's take on all of this, she was also hungry. As she listened, she ate.

"The history is told that this land comes from the wants and desires of those who enter into it, but only a chosen few who enter can decide its overall path." Putting his cup down, he continued, "Many creatures—and yes even humans—enter this place for one reason or another, finding the path that their true heart's desire. Most of them find their paradise in one form or another and stay here quite contented for the rest of their days. Others of us were born here and remain here. You, Sarah, are the one for this time we are in. You will be the one who decides our overall fate."

Sarah wiped her mouth with the napkin and said, "Forgive me for having to ask, but what is this place anyway? And how did I actually wind up here? And why me?"

Arron stood up, reached for Sarah's hand, and led her over to a large window. Below, the city was hustling with life. "This place has never had a name but the Dark Land. The world here, as a whole, is called Meddillion. How you came to be here is much simpler than why you were chosen. You came to Meddillion because you—like many others—were searching for something you couldn't find where you were. Some people come here, and before they even notice that anything is out of place, their desire goes.

They go back to their lives, never knowing the splendor of Meddillion." Touching her face, he said, "Your heart burns for what you seek."

Sarah emotionally understood what Arron was saying. When she began her walkabout, she was looking for something. Her heart felt trapped then, and her stomach was tied in knots. With Arron, even with so many questions, she didn't have those feelings. She just nodded and enjoyed his comforting touch. He was all she could see at that moment.

Arron's attention was directed to a commotion outside the window.

A man in uniform entered the room, bowed his head quickly, and said, "Sire, I implore you to come quickly!"

Arron looked to him and then back to Sarah. "Please forgive me." He kissed her hand softly and followed the man out the door.

From the window, Sarah watched the streets become chaotic with many men and beasts in uniform. When Arron and the man walked briskly down the path, Sarah caught herself admiring Arron's build and demeanor. He was handsome, and Sarah felt drawn to him even more.

ᴂ Chapter 8

Turning from the window, Sarah felt fresh with the spirit of adventure. She decided to visit the stables while she awaited Arron's return. She would have to remember how to navigate through the main house and the village to get there. She only remembered that it was on her right coming in. In theory, it should be on her left if she went the opposite way.

Out in the hall, Sarah was impressed by the decor—and even more so by the way people reacted to her. Everyone she passed bowed their heads as they did with Arron. She wondered what gave them the idea that she was as privileged. Did they think she was the *one*? She figured, like everything else there, it would be revealed at some point. As she walked onto the street, Sarah felt as beautiful as the day was bright.

She made her way past the parlors, stores, and saloons. The stables were right where she remembered. She thought a stable so large would have a lot of people milling about, but it was only the horses in their stalls.

Sarah walked down the main walkway, and the odor of horses comforted her. She had adored horses since childhood. When the large, white stallion in the first stable saw her, it stood and kicked the air wildly, startling her for a moment. When the horse settled down a bit, Sarah could have sworn it was smiling. Remembering that things there were not as she knew them back home, she returned the awkward smile and moved on.

Twelve stalls on either side ran down the main corridor. In the center, there were two smaller halls with three stalls on each side. Each one held a beautifully groomed and quite content horse.

Sarah came to the crossway of the aisles and decided to go down the one to her right. The first horse was sleeping, and the second was eating.

The loveliest creature she had ever seen was in the third stall. It stood proud and looked at Sarah with soft, brown eyes. As Sarah approached the gate, so did the horse. Sarah gently put her hand on the horse's forehead, slowly unlatched the gate that separated them, and went into the stall. She couldn't take her eyes off the fabulous creature's coat. "Who are you?" she asked.

With the crash of a pail and the scuffling of some hay, an old man said, "That's Spirit." He threw some hay into the bin in front of them. "You oughtta be careful. These horses get their names for a reason, ya know. The last one who got too close to Spirit here met with the maker of their own spirit, they did."

"She hardly seems like the type." Sarah didn't take her eyes off Spirit.

"Well, take your chances if you will, but it not be on my head when I have to report you dead." The man grinned at Sarah in an unforgiving manner and shuffled off to the next stall to continue his daily rounds.

"Spirit is your name. My name is Sarah." The warmth of friendship she had not felt in a long time filled her heart. "I will find out if I can see you again. We have a connection, you and I."

Almost in reply, Spirit looked directly at Sarah. The horse turned her neck so her head was touching Sarah's shoulder. The moment seemed to last forever.

Through the window in Spirit's stall, Sarah heard men talking. At first, she tried not to listen, but her interest in what they were saying grew quickly. She stood underneath the window and listened.

"He went to go speak with the general."

"Do ya think it's gonna be soon?"

"It can't be. We're not ready, and the girl isn't prepared."

"I still don't get why we have to fight to keep this one here."

Sarah's ears perked up.

"It'll be the way he wants it. And that's what he wants, so that's what we fight for. You know better than to ask those types of questions. Come on. We gotta get our gear ready just in case."

"Why now? Nothin's been declared yet."

"Another question?"

Sarah heard a smack.

When the men moved on, Sarah paused, standing very still. She was starting to understand. Touching Spirit again, she whispered, "That *she* they were talking about is me, isn't it?" She didn't expect an answer, but with a nod and a whinny, Sarah got the impression that Spirit knew it was.

"How I do wish you could really speak to me." Sarah was overwhelmed by the need to ride Spirit. She unlatched the gate and led Spirit down the narrow path to the back entrance. "How about a ride?" she said with a giggle.

Saddling Spirit up was a very exciting few minutes for her. She had not saddled a horse up by herself since she was a child. Spirit was very patient and stood still as Sarah fumbled with the harness and buckles. Soon enough, Spirit was ready—and so was Sarah. She grabbed Spirit's lush, black mane and straddled the saddle like an old pro. With a click of her heels and a *tsk* from her lips, they were off like lightning.

The back courtyard exited into a vast prairie. Sarah could see a wall surrounding the area, but it wasn't for quite some distance. She egged Spirit on to run faster. Spirit complied with ease, and they raced toward the wall. Sarah started to get a little concerned at their speed and pulled back on Spirit's reins, but Spirit did not respond. Faster and faster she ran—straight at the wall. Sarah thought that the horse had gone mad and remembered what the keeper had said.

Something started moving under her legs as they ran. The saddle came up off the horse's back a little, and something pushed Sarah's legs out of position. Feeling a bit wobbly and still concerned about the wall, Sarah made one last effort to stop Spirit. Just as Sarah pulled back on the reins, the ground left them—and the wall went right underneath their feet.

Sarah could not believe what was happening. They were flying. Only in a fairy tale could that be true. Spirit lifted off like a cloud on a windy day, and the two of them soared through the air. She felt happier than she had been in a long time.

From where they flew, Sarah could see the layout of the city. She could see the balcony of her room. Vast plains and thick forests surrounded most of the area except for a hint of blue over the eastern horizon. Sarah guessed it was an ocean, but it was too far away to be sure.

Near the north horizon, she noticed a significant change. There was a light among many trees. When she headed toward it, she looked down into center of the Dark City.

Arron was staring up at her. He looked angry.

She pulled on Spirit's reins, and they landed next to Arron and three of his guards.

When Sarah and Spirit landed, Arron's face softened. He smiled and said, "I must leave the city for a little while." He helped Sarah dismount. "Would you, for your own safety, promise me you will remain within the city walls?" With a smirk, he added, "Preferably on the ground."

Sarah took Spirit's reins and began to walk her back to the stable. She looked at Arron and shrugged. "I think I can do that for you." With all she had overheard and Arron's look of concern, Sarah did not find it such an outrageous request.

After Spirit was safely in her stall, Arron led Sarah to the front of the stable. He took her hand, kissed it, and said, "I will be back as soon as I'm able."

Sarah asked, "You make that sound as if it will be a long time."

Arron looked deeply at her and replied, "I shouldn't think it would be, but one never knows." He smiled and walked away with three guards.

Looking out onto the street, Sarah chose to turn away

from the main house. She walked past men pushing carts, women leading children, and other women just hanging about. Across the road, men watched the women hanging about. There were fruit carts and butchers bustling about on all the streets. It was not a little place, and there was something going on everywhere. When she reached a tavern with two swinging doors, she decided to go in.

She was hit with the ripe aroma of beer, sweat, and tobacco smoke. The cool breeze from outside moved the air around enough to make it tolerable.

All the stools were available at the bar, and she walked up and claimed one.

The bartender came up to her and asked, "Are you sure you're in the right place, miss?"

"Do you serve cold drinks here?" Sarah asked.

"Aye." The man nodded.

"Then, yes, I believe I am. I'll have whatever cold drink you're serving today."

"Comin' up, miss." He walked to the other end of the long bar.

Sarah looked around at all the things that hung behind the bar. There was a long knife with a leather handle and a wanted sign with a picture of an incredibly ugly man. Sarah looked at the face again after she saw the reward amount. She decided she could not miss a man who looked like that.

The mirror behind the bar, which was as long as the bar itself, was decorated with beautifully hand-carved wood. After a few moments, Sarah realized it was the design of the woodwork of Gropal.

Her eyes wandered to the reflection in the mirror, but something was not right. The reflection was dark and eerie.

The sun had faded outside, but with the gray hue, she could see leaves blowing around outside.

A man at the corner table met her gaze. His eyes glowed red in their sockets. She looked at her reflection in the mirror, and with a bloodcurdling scream, she covered her eyes with her hands.

The bartender came over and put her drink down on the counter. "You okay?"

Sarah expected to see the worst, but it was only the bartender. She looked at him and then at the glass. She quickly took it and drank half of it. After putting it down, she said, "I'm okay. Thanks for the drink."

Sarah had the same feeling as when Arron gave her the drink in the cabin. Her skin warmed up, her fears subsided, and she felt calm. Sarah looked up at the mirror again, and all was as it should be.

She was concerned about the visions she was having. None of them had been pleasant. Why was she having them? She had never had visions until she came into that world. What could they be about?

Sarah chuckled as she took another sip. She was thinking about how funny it was to stumble upon an alternate world as amazing as this and be cursed with horrible visions instead of happy ones. The more she drank, the better she felt—and the farther away the fears and doubts became. Things with Sarah were fine again for the moment.

After a while, a sturdy figure in a brown cloak walked through the swinging doors. The figure walked straight up to the dingy bar and stood a foot away from her.

Sarah tried to focus on the stranger's face. When she finally made it out, she realized it was Sar.

Sarah was very excited to see him. She jumped from her stool—with a stagger—and went to embrace him.

He grabbed her by her upper arms and sat her back in her seat. With a nod to the barkeep, her drink was removed from the counter. Sar covered her with his cloak and began to walk with her back to the main house.

As they walked, he said, "I heard you were here."

"From who?" Sarah answered with a giggle.

"Tinbe," he answered as he pulled on her arm.

Sarah let out a sigh. "That Tinbe can be quite the little pest, can't he?"

Sar stopped in his tracks and stopped Sarah. "A pest?" he asked with a sour expression.

"Yes, a pest. He seems to have followed me since I arrived in this fantasy world I've managed to land in," she said with her arms swirling about.

"That's because you are who you are—and you are as important as you are," he said with a serious look.

Sarah returned his glance, mirroring his stern stance, and then she burst out in drunken laughter. "I am who I am is true enough, but important as all of this? I think not." As she started to walk away, Sar grabbed her arm again.

At the entrance to the main house, Sar removed his cloak to show off the military uniform underneath. With that uniform, he would be free to take Sarah to her room. He let her lead the way.

Once in the room, Sar asked Sarah for her goblet. She pointed to the cabinet and flopped down onto the bed.

Sar walked to the cabinet and found her bag. He took out the goblet and filled it with water from a pouch around his shoulder. "Drink." He held out the cup.

"I think I've done enough of that for one day. Thank you." She pushed her hair back over her pale face.

"Please, Miss Sarah. This will help bring you back a bit. Drink." He motioned for her to take the goblet.

Sarah took it from Sar and drank. Within a few minutes, she began to sober up.

Sar brought her bag over and asked her to show him the other items she had been given. "The medallion and the pot." He pushed the bag toward her.

Dazed a bit, she asked, "What about them?"

"Do you still possess them?" He nudged the bag closer to her.

"Sure, they've been in there the whole time." She took them out, handed them to Sar, and put her head back on the pillow. She was starting to feel a bit better, but she was still exhausted and a bit nauseous.

"Miss Sarah, it would be wise of you to keep these with you. And, if I may, please eat from the pot and drink from the goblet every day. The food you are served here is poison."

Sarah opened an eye and lifted her head. "Poison? But I've already eaten here and drank what they've served, and I feel just fine. What do you mean by poison?"

"It will poison your mind and your spirit."

Sarah, feeling a little better, sat up in the bed and said, "Can I ask you something?"

Sar motioned for her to continue with a nod.

"If I'm not supposed to be here—and this place is so dangerous and I am so important to you and Taurik and Tinbe and God knows who else—why don't you just take me out of here?"

Sar's face tightened with sadness. He looked up at her and said, "Because you chose to come here—and only you can choose to leave."

Sar packed up the three items and reminded her to use them as he had suggested.

Sarah nodded, and in her spinning mind, she knew she had a lot to think about. Right then, she was too tired. When Sar left, she fell asleep alone.

Darkness took over Sarah's mind, and the reality of her unrealistic day slipped away into an even stranger place. She found herself standing under a dark, ominous sky, hearing snarls and drums and the clanging of metal. She looked through the haze and saw a mountain of darkness with a man standing at its peak. He was wrapped in a red warrior's uniform. The wind swirled around him as he lifted his arms. She could see a black hole at his feet. Sarah could make out moans, sorrowful calls, and the voices of ghosts and souls of creatures—men and women who were once like she was. They were whirling and swirling around the mountain and the man. They ended up falling into the blackness of the hole at his feet. Even though the pull of the hole seemed great, the man in red was not moved. She focused closer on the man and saw parts of his face. He was enjoying the scene and growing stronger with every soul that entered the abyss.

With a sudden change of direction, Sarah had a different view. It was another mountain, but it was covered in light. At the base, there was a vast ocean of colorful flowers, and a lovely song covered the area. There were soft breezes, and she could see souls much like the ones from the other mountain, but they were not moaning.

They were singing and floating all around the mountain in much slower spirals.

At the top of the mountain, a man with white hair that blew gently in the breezes raised one of his arms. He held a staff with a blue crystal at its top. His robe was white with gold and silver weaved together with the colors of the flowers beneath him. He stood strong and smiled. Sarah had never seen such a beautiful place, and her soul felt at ease.

Deeper into her slumber she went, and as night ended, Sarah was whipped around again by a sudden gust. It pulled her over to the dark mountain, and she was sucked up toward the top. She started to scream, and as she came close to the red warrior, she could see his face. Sarah was silenced. It was Arron.

Sarah sat straight up in her bed and realized it was a dream. The whole place felt like a dream to her, and she was momentarily disoriented. She pushed the covers off and sat at the edge of the bed. Shaking her head, she said, "What the hell was that?"

Sarah walked over to the vanity and patted down her face, neck, and hands. She sat in front of the mirror and brushed her hair. Her mind wandered to Sar. Had he been there as she remembered? She knew she had been quite drunk the night before, but could she have imagined him altogether?

When she returned the brush to her bag, her hand hit the goblet. She remembered Sar's warning. Sarah didn't know why, but she trusted him. She did not think the food and drink in the castle were poisonous, but she thought she had better keep her bag with her from then on. Just in case.

Out of the corner of her eye, Sarah spotted the beautiful dress Vente had made for her. It had been cleaned, pressed, and mended. Sarah took it off the hanger and contemplated putting it on. When she looked in the mirror, she was struck by how beautiful the sleek dress made her appear. She decided against changing and put the dress in her bag.

Sarah decided she didn't need a few of the items that were weighing her down. She took them out and set them on the table next to the water bowl. She closed her bag, flung it over her shoulder, and walked to the balcony to see what the day was like. As her eyes adjusted to the sunshine, the breeze started to blow through her hair. She was momentarily taken back to the patio of her hotel room where she had been so eager to start her vacation.

When she opened her eyes, the reality hit that she was not on vacation anymore—and the world she found herself in was very real. It sunk in that she was in a place that she didn't know how to get home from. She started to wonder if she would ever see her mother again. The sadness of that thought brought emptiness to her heart.

❧ Chapter 9

SARAH WALKED THROUGH HER BEDROOM DOOR AND CLOSED it behind her quietly. She began to explore the many hallways of the main house. As one hallway led into another, she realized she had only seen a small part of the main house.

She walked down the hallways and admired the artwork. Most of it was beautiful, but some pieces were downright frightening. They seemed to come off the walls as she passed them.

One of the paintings at the end of a long passage was fenced off. Sarah walked up to it, being careful that no one was behind her. She looked at the face of the man on the canvas. Sarah's heart started to race, and she felt dizzy. The weight of a thousand soldiers was on her, which forced her to step back from the rope.

When she regained her composure, Sarah decided to see if her visions could be controlled. She took a step toward the rope and reached out her hand. As soon as she touched the canvas, she saw Taurik in a battle of a thousand men. He had been bloodied, but the blood was not his own. Taurik knelt down and touched the body of the woman warrior at his feet. She was drenched in blood from a mortal wound to her chest. He stood up, raised his sword, and screamed a battle cry that spanned time. Taurik left the scene, and hundreds of surviving warriors followed him.

Sarah tried to concentrate on where they were going. She couldn't see very well, but she did see the mountain of light from her dream.

When she let go of the canvas and mentally returned to where she stood, Sarah was left with a feeling of defeat and then the feeling of victory that came directly from the heart of Taurik. She knew it for certain.

Sarah knew she had to get to White Mountain, and she had to learn more about the castle and the people who lived there. Walking away from the painting, she made her way out a side door that emptied onto the street.

Combating a feeling of deep loss as she walked, Sarah realized how deeply she missed Taurik. She did not understand how that could be possible since she hardly knew him. She remembered leaving him at the camp that night and regretted not being nicer. Sarah wondered if she would see him again and hoped that she would.

Looking around for a way to go, Sarah spotted the little girl. The girl's eyes widened, and she ran the other way. Not knowing why the girl would have a reason to be frightened, Sarah followed.

Passing a number of stores and row houses, Sarah caught sight of the girl running through an open door to a house on the corner. Walking up to it slowly, she noted the amount of care that had been taken to keep the old building in tip-top condition. The stoop was freshly swept, the few flowers that hung from the porch were well cared for, and the old rocking chair in the corner had a fresh coat of paint. It looked comfortable and inviting.

"May I help you?" a loud, unkind voice said from the doorway.

Sarah spun around in fear. Instead of a giant to match the voice, it was an old, dark-skinned woman in a housedress. Her gray hair was up, and the woman's wrinkles told stories of years of worry and strain.

Sarah found it difficult to get a word out. The old lady's tone startled her so much she couldn't find her breath. Finally, she was able to say, "The little girl … I was—"

"You was what?" the lady said loudly. She took a step out of the doorway and onto the porch.

Sarah was tired of the confusion and not knowing who she could—or couldn't—trust. When the back of her legs hit the rocking chair she had been admiring, she sat quickly.

Sarah thought the old lady was going to grab her ear and throw her off the porch. Instead, the lady came over, lifted her out of the chair, and ushered her inside.

The screen door slapped shut behind them, and Sarah was led through a large kitchen and into a back parlor. The old lady closed the door behind them and said, "My name is Sandanti. Who are you, child?" There was a pause that was apparently too long for Sandanti because she added, "Well, speak up. Who are you?"

"Oh. I'm sorry." Sarah sat up in the soft chair. "I'm Sarah."

Sandanti took a seat.

Sarah said, "I was following the little girl … she seemed frightened of me and there really is no need to be … and—"

"Oh, Sarah, is it? That would explain the dress." Sandanti smiled as she sat back in her chair.

Sarah looked around the room and suddenly felt very overdressed. She was about to get up when Sandanti started to laugh a heartily.

Sarah had no idea what she was laughing at, but it was contagious. Sarah felt a smile come across her face—her first spontaneous smile in days.

Between breaths, Sandanti said, "Oh, my child, I am so sorry. Please forgive me, but you are an open book, aren't you?" She started to get out of her chair.

As Sandanti came up to her, Sarah grabbed her pack and placed it on her lap. Sarah pulled away when Sandanti reached out to grab her hand.

"No need to not trust me. Let me show you." Sandanti took Sarah's hand and led her to the mirror on the back wall.

"Look there. Do you see?" She pointed.

Sarah saw the reflection of a woman in a ripped black dress. Her hair was a mess, and her face was pale. She touched her cheek and felt her snarled hair. "How?" she muttered.

After a minute Sandanti said, "Honey, don't be too frightened that you couldn't see it before. Most never see the truth at all. You are one of the lucky ones."

"I don't feel so lucky," Sarah replied, still looking herself over in the mirror.

Sandanti left for a minute, and Sarah's mind flooded with despair. How could she have thought she was beautiful? How could she have thought she was charming? How could she be such a mess? The truth was before her. She was a mess.

Sandanti came back, put her arm around Sarah, and said, "Oh, my child, you are beautiful."

Instead of being shocked, Sarah just felt tired. She looked at Sandanti and said, "What now?"

Sandanti smiled gently and pulled Sarah's hair back behind her shoulders. "Now, child, your *trueness* has spoken to you, and you have heard it. Let's fix you up, huh?" She picked up Sarah's bag and led her down a narrow hallway to an empty bedroom.

"My first suggestion would be for you to put on something you truly feel comfortable in."

Sarah felt the softness of the dress she was wearing and looked down at it. It was tattered. She certainly didn't feel comfortable in it anymore. The only clothes to choose from were in her bag. Sarah thought about the dress that Vente had made for her. She put her bag down on the bed and looked over her shoulder. Sandanti had left the room. Sarah reached into the bag and felt the soft linen.

She held it up, looked it over, and slowly lowered it onto the bed. She didn't feel that Vente's dress, as beautiful as it may have been, would have honestly answered that question. What did she feel comfortable in? Sarah was out of options—until an open closet door caught her eye. It was filled with clothes of all sizes, colors, and styles.

From behind, Sandanti said, "Go ahead, darlin'. Try some on." She closed the door behind her to give Sarah some privacy.

Sarah scanned the clothing and couldn't remember a time when figuring out what to wear had been so confusing. Then she realized the question was tripping her up. For years, Sarah had worn what others thought looked good, what others had given her, or what was most convenient. Sarah sat back on the bed to collect her thoughts. She was sure the task was not that difficult. She tried on outfit after outfit; nothing really looked bad on her, but she was not comfortable in any of them. When she tried on the last few articles of clothing, she finally found what she felt comfortable in.

Sarah looked herself over in the mirror and smiled. The brown cotton pants hung nicely around her waist and fell even nicer down her legs, coming to a halt below her knees. The top was ivory. It was plain, but the natural wrinkles in the fabric made it stand out. She decided to put on a loose undershirt. The one she had was shredded and worn—and she honestly hadn't liked it to begin with. The sandals that Vente had given her were still perfect.

Once she was all put together, she sat on the bed and contemplated taking a nap. She remembered her journal and took it out. She had to dig a little to locate the pencil, and she found a spot to write.

> Day #?
> I am still in this place, but now this is a new place from the last time I wrote. So much has happened. I think I've been here only a few weeks, but it feels as though I've been here for years. To be honest, I don't really know anymore. Everything seems to be dragging together.
> At the moment, I am in an old woman's house. Sandanti seems to be real nice and has honesty in her eyes. Not like I'd trust

myself to know what that was, but I think it
is anyway. I looked different in her mirror.
Horrible, in fact. Can't believe I hadn't seen
it before. I am now washed and dressed in
comfortable clothes, and I do feel worlds
better.

This house seems unusually airy for
this city. I am glad to be here. Actually,
I'm glad to be anywhere but where I was.
I was lied to, I think. Well, I'm not sure,
but I know that it wasn't right there in the
castle, and Sandanti says I should stay here
for a bit.

I'm a little afraid to follow someone else
in this place, but as I've felt before, I truly
don't know if I have a choice at this point if I
should ever see home again. I am still eager
to meet the little girl. I haven't seen her since
I arrived, but I know she's here.

She shut the book and smelled something delicious
coming from the other room. Sarah followed the aromas
to the kitchen and asked, "Can I help?"

Sandanti looked over her shoulder and answered,
"Well, well, doesn't that just fit you perfect. Yes, honey,
you can help. Grab those plates and set them on the table
in the far room. I'll be out in just a minute."

Sarah took the plates and did as she was told. The table
was to be set for six. Sarah wondered who would be there.
She felt a little anxious about it, but she was not sure why.
No sooner did that feeling come than it left.

Sandanti entered the room with a steaming turkey pie. She put it on the table and motioned for Sarah to take a seat. She went to the door and rang an old metal bell. On her way back to the table, she stopped in the kitchen. When she finally sat down, she put down a beautiful chocolate cake.

The table filled up quickly with four rosy-cheeked children, including the little girl. Sandanti took her place at the head of the table; with nothing more than a look, the children fell silent. They bowed their heads, and Sandanti gave thanks for the food they were about to eat. She also gave thanks for many other things. When she was done, everyone waited for her to serve the food.

The dishes seemed to take forever to reach Sarah. She felt like she was never going to get to taste the delicious treats in front of her.

Little was said for the first few minutes of the fine supper, but as their bellies began to fill up, the chatter started. Most of it was directed at Sarah but not *to* her.

Before Sarah could get too self-conscious, Sandanti said, "I would like you all to meet Sarah—and one of you to meet officially." There was another little shuffle of sound. "Aren't we all very shy today? Go on. Introduce yourselves."

The oldest boy sat up straight and looked around at the others. "I'm Peter," he said proudly. He nudged the boy next to him, and it continued.

In a much smaller voice, the younger lad said, "I'm Verd." Verd had darker skin and a scaly clef, like that of a crocodile, on his forehead. A physical trait found on the pre-adolescent warriors of his people.

Down the table it went. "I'm Frana." Without hesitation, she pointed to the smallest girl and said, "That's Tarra."

Sandanti gave a water-choked cough. When she caught her breath, she said, "Okay, children, I may remind you that all of us are going picking tomorrow." A big cheer erupted around the table. "We're going pickin'. You all need to get to bed now." That one was followed by a long sigh. "Come on now. Get goin'."

Everyone started to get up, including Sarah.

Sandanti said, "Not you, Sarah. You stay with me for now."

Sarah looked around at the kids, but Tarra was the only one who paid any attention to the last command. She looked back until the older girl grabbed her wrist and yanked her out of the hallway.

Sarah finished clearing off the table, and Sandanti put the kettle on and washed the dishes. Sarah liked the sound of softly running water and the gentle clanking of dishes.

Sandanti pointed to some smaller place settings and asked Sarah to set the table for the two of them for some tea.

As Sarah took out the dishes, she heard a soft song coming from the kitchen. It was lovely. She finished setting the dishes, sat down, closed her eyes, and listened.

"Coming round … comin' round. The songs of little ones comin' round. Through the trees, out to the seas, the songs of our own are comin' round."

Sandanti wiped her hands and joined Sarah at the table. She stopped humming only after the candle in front of them was lit. With a deep breath, she sat back in her chair. "So, Miss Sarah, I would imagine your mind is whirling with things to be answered." After sipping her tea, she continued, "I will do my best to answer if you ask."

Sarah was faced with another person who could tell she

was confused. Sandanti was willing to remedy the situation. A number of people had offered similar conversations to Sarah with little result. She nervously took a sip of tea and said, "I'm not sure I know where to start." She put the saucer back on the table gently.

Sandanti smiled and said, "I was always told to start at the beginning."

"You make that sound so simple." Sarah tried to get her thoughts together.

"Things usually are. We tend to complicate them," Sandanti said.

"Why don't we start with where we are right now? This house? It's different from the rest of the city. And why does it seem that you are the only person to see the measure of my confusion?" Sarah waited for an answer.

"My child, hasn't anyone told you anything?"

Sarah continued to look at Sandanti, blinking a few times. If she distracted herself too much, the moment for answers might pass.

Sandanti continued, "This house that you sit in now has been, for generations, the house where the *undecideds* have found their true selves. The city you are in is home to it because the souls that don't belong to the Dark Lord sometimes find themselves here—despite their wishes—by accident, invitation, or birth. This house and the ones who have run it are here to make sure that those souls have a chance to find their way to King Rika and the White Mountain of Eslinar. Without this station, you and the others would be lost to the darkness, trapped, or worse."

Sarah asked, "The Dark Lord is Arron?"

"Ah, yes, you know him by name. You fell rather

far. Your spirit is strong for you to have fought your way through my doors."

"I did no fighting." Sarah shook her head.

"More than you know, my child. Those feelings of uncertainty, the moments when your cheeks flushed, the times you felt that something was not right whether it be through your gut, your mind, or your eyes—or even in your ability to see."

"How do you know about my visions?" Sarah asked.

"Couldn't be certain, but your mother had them too. It would be natural that you would have them as well."

"My mother?" Sarah's mind started to spin. She cupped her head in her palms. "Every time I think things are just about to make sense, something else is thrown out at me that just messes my head up even worse than it was before. What are you talking about?"

Sandanti poured more tea and said, "I suppose I should start at the beginning since you seem to know even less than I thought." She leaned forward and took Sarah's hand. "I see this is a new world to you. You must know where you came from if you are to know where you are going ... they are linked. The world you came from is new compared to the one you are in now. The world you know began when some folks left this one—some voluntarily and some not. As time went on, the barrier between the two worlds grew. One day, only this world knew of them both."

"This is impossible." Sarah shook her head again.

"Sometimes the truth is stranger than make-believe." She sipped her tea and waited for a signal to continue.

Sandanti did not want to burden Sarah with more information than she could handle, but she knew that if

Sarah's quest was to be successful—not to mention that it would benefit the whole existence of both worlds if she were—Sarah had to be given the tools. Sandanti believed, against the decision of the council, that the biggest tool a young woman could have was the truth. But she also knew that too much truth, too fast could be quite damaging.

Sarah wanted desperately to get up and run. Instead, she took a deep breath and followed it with some tea. Sarah would do anything to hear some truth and some answers. "Please, I'm fine. Go on."

Sandanti nodded and said, "From the beginning of time, there has always been a struggle between the right and the wrong. There have been times of great peace, and there have been times of great wars. As with everything, there is something that—or someone who—decides that. Sometimes people or creatures decide that only for themselves, but there are very rare times where one individual or one creature can decide that for all living things. In my lifetime, there has only been one such person. That person was your mother."

Sandanti paused, took a breath, and said, "Your mother was found in a clearing near the base of White Mountain. She was just a baby. She was taken in by a couple who had wanted children but had none. As she grew up in the shadows of White Mountain, only the crown and the council knew she was the one of light. As you are. As your mother grew, she learned of her powers and of her own truths. The tale is simple really: Her beauty caught the eye of the prince. They were introduced and fell in love. Not too long after, they were wed. For some time, they lived peacefully and happily—and happier still were they to learn that they were to soon have a new life to look after."

Sarah looked up and met Sandanti's eyes.

"Yes, you," Sandanti said with a nod.

Sarah started to tear up. A tear rolled down her cheek and fell on the table. "Why didn't she tell me?" she whispered through quivering lips.

Sandanti took a small spoon and stirred her tea. "It was a very happy time until word came that the Dark Army was growing strong. Your mother knew she could not stay in the castle. Eslinar would soon be under attack, and she had to save her child. Her child was the tie, the landmark to all things good. Her child, you, was born with both noble and spiritual blood, and if allowed to live, you could and probably would rejoin all beings in this land in harmony. With the help of some of the subjects and her devoted husband, she found the boundary between worlds and crossed over to the world you knew as home. She vowed to raise you in that world and keep the other from you so that you would not be found out."

Sarah's face went pale. "Are you telling me that my mother is a spiritual being of light—and my father is of noble blood, which to my understanding means immortal here?"

Sandanti let out a hefty laugh. "No. Immortal would mean he would live forever and ever after, and if that were so, there would be no balance in this or any other world. Noble lines live—give or take—about three hundred years as you would count them."

"Three hundred?" Sarah yelped. "But then if they eventually die like the rest, why is it so important? What difference does it make? Why does the fact that I am here make any difference to anyone?" Sarah stood and began to pace.

Sandanti ushered Sarah into the living room next to the small fireplace. She nestled into her favorite chair and said, "Imagine, child, if you can, the amount of information one being learns during a lifetime. It's a shame really that most of that knowledge is lost when the being passes on. All that's left are writings and assumptions about those writings. Now imagine living long enough to learn and create the writings and to be able to pass down the ideals, ideas, and questions. Most nobles have known and have had the power to heal minds, bodies, and spirits for centuries. Their knowledge is more vast than I can relate or even know."

"So how does that relate to my mother and me?" Sarah stood by the fireplace.

"It relates to you because you are of both lines, a common link between the nobles and all other beings. You are the only one who can bring peace to our world for good." Sandanti's eyes grew dark. "Or you'll be the one to ruin it." After a moment's pause, they locked eyes. "It all depends on where your heart is."

After a tense moment, Sarah took a deep breath and started to laugh so hard that she crumbled into the chair across from Sandanti.

Sandanti looked stunned.

When Sarah regained her composure, she said, "No pressure, huh?"

They laughed together for a long time.

☙ Chapter 10

WHEN MORNING CAME, SARAH FELT MUCH BETTER THAN SHE had in many days. She awoke in a warm bed in a warm room. The sun was shining, a smell of food came from the kitchen, and she could make out the sound of laughter in the distance. She had not realized how much she missed that sound. Sarah got herself together, took a deep breath, and quietly enjoyed the wonderful aromas for a few minutes.

In the kitchen, Sandanti was masterfully cooking breakfast for everyone. When Sarah got to the table, Sandanti set down the last basket of rolls, went over to the door, and rang the bell. In under a minute, the room was filled with the sound of scuffling feet on the hardwood floor. The chairs filled up with children, and before Sarah knew it, all four of them were sitting with their hands clasped and their eyes down.

Sandanti smiled as she joined them. "We thank you, Great Creator, for all things wonderful in this world, and we ask that you give us the strength we need to continue on whatever path it is you have chosen for us."

Sarah bowed her head.

The wonderful meal filled Sarah's belly and heart with

joy. Soon enough, there was a lot of conversation going around the table, and it was all about Sarah. She began to feel a little uncomfortable.

Sandanti finished the last of her eggs, wiped her mouth, stood, and raised her glass. "I would like to make an introduction and a toast."

The children and Sarah raised their glasses and listened.

"I would like to introduce all of you again to Sarah. She has traveled far and came here as you have. A toast to all of us: may the Great One know our hearts, may the sun be our friend," she looked at the children with a sheepish grin, and they all chimed in with great joy, "and may the pickin' be plenty!" They chugged their drinks, and Sarah joined them with delight.

After the meal, the children put their plates in the kitchen without being told. Sarah had never met such well-mannered children, and they held onto their childish excitement about everything. They all scattered to prepare for the picking adventure.

Tarra came back and sat down next to Sarah. "You seem nice. Do you want to play?"

Before Sarah could answer, Sandanti came in and said, "Tarra, I would like to speak with Sarah. Go on outside now."

Tarra nodded, smiled at Sarah, and left the room without another word.

Sandanti ushered Sarah into the parlor, but it looked different than it had the night before. The sun came in through the open widows, and the air was filled with the smell of fresh flowers instead of burning embers. Sarah sat in the same seat.

Sandanti said, "I wanted to let you know ahead of time what you will be coming up against if you decide to come with us on our journey to White Mountain."

"Decide? But you already told me that my mother—"

"Yes, yes your mother lived there—and your father was prince—but that does not mean that you necessarily will follow their path. You, Miss Sarah, have to decide for yourself."

"Why would I doubt it? That's where I want to go."

"You seem very certain for a girl who was almost struck down by the curse of the Dark Lord." Sandanti looked up over her reading glasses. "Or have you already forgotten your state when you arrived at my doorstep yesterday?"

Sarah got up out of the chair and went to the window. Looking out into the garden, she remembered the mirror at the tavern. A memory flashed of the night in Arron's house. She felt the warmth from when she was in his arms. Her mind came back to where she stood, and her cheeks began to flush.

"He can be quite intoxicating, can't he?" Sandanti said softly as she began to work on her knitting.

Before Sarah could say anything else, Sandanti put down her knitting needles and walked over to the window. Putting her hands on Sarah's shoulders, she said, "Why don't you go and play with the children today. We don't leave for picking until later. Have fun, clear your head, and maybe your true path will show itself to you."

Sarah nodded, smiled, and went out to the garden. All the children besides Tarra were laughing and playing.

Tarra was sitting by herself near a small pond. She was bent over the low rock boundary that kept the water in. As

Sarah got a little closer, she saw that Tarra was not playing with the fish or the water. She was looking at her reflection.

Sarah said, "Whatcha doin'?"

Tarra giggled. "I'm lookin' at my face. Wanna see?" She pointed into the water.

Sarah knelt down next to Tarra and looked into the water. She could not believe what she saw. Tarra's reflection didn't show a fair-skinned, blonde girl. The scaly, gray child could have been Sar's sister or daughter. Sarah had to look again at the little girl in front of her to make sure she was not losing her sight as well as her mind. When she looked back into the water, the gray reflection was still there.

Tarra noticed Sarah's confusion, which was becoming increasingly hard to hide, and started to giggle again. "You're not used to things around here are you?"

Sarah answered, "No, I guess I'm not." She sat back against the rocks, took a deep breath, and looked at Tarra. Sarah realized that Tarra did not find her surroundings weird or confusing. Other than their ages, the biggest difference between them was that Tarra had been in that strange place her whole life. It was normal to her. She'd never known anything different.

Without another thought, Sarah said, "Why are all of our reflections different from what we see?"

Tarra took Sarah's hand in her own and pointed at the reflection. "See? You see who you are on the inside. You know ... who you really are."

Sarah said, "Do you know a young man by the name of Sar?"

"Of course!" Tarra answered with a big smile. "He's my uncle. How do you know Uncle Sar?"

"He helped save me." She knew her answer simplified things a bit.

Tarra smiled, pushed her hair out of her eyes, and poked Sarah on the arm. "Tag. You're it!" She ran away as fast as her little legs could take her.

Before Sarah knew what had happened, she found herself running through the garden, around the house, and out into the field. They were laughing and rolling and laughing some more as they fell into a pile of hay by the back fence.

The sound of Sandanti's bell filled the air. Sarah and Tarra looked at each other and realized they were very hungry. They chased each other into the house, and as the scent of honey filled the air, they washed their hands and sat at the table. Tarra pulled up the chair next to Sarah. Sarah felt wonderful, and the food only made her feel better.

When the meal was over, Sandanti reminded the children about going picking the next day. She instructed them to get their bags packed and meet in the parlor for story time.

All of them shouted "Hurray!" They ran out of the room and packed their belongings into small satchels.

Sarah went into the room and packed her bag. She repacked her hairbrush, hair tie, toothbrush, feminine products, and her tattered clothes. She decided to leave out some of the worst ones. Next in was Vente's dress. It was so beautifully simple that Sarah thought she might have an occasion to wear it again somewhere down the line. She folded it gently and put it between two other items. She packed Tinbe's pot, which she had not mentioned to anyone since the campfire with Taurik and Sar. Sarah carefully tied the medallion around the bottom of the goblet to ensure its safety. She remembered the medallion was strong enough to keep some enemies at bay. *What was it that he told me to say?* Her mind's focus went back to her encounter with the Jagruts. *Telgot de nomtera.* She removed it from the bottom of the goblet and slipped it over her head. Sarah decided to keep the medallion around her neck from then on.

She took out her journal, closed the bedroom door, and sat on the bed.

> I don't know what day it is anymore.
>
> Perhaps I've waited too long since my last entry. I don't think I can even start to write down everything that has happened since, so I will write where I am now. I followed a little girl Tarra to this house. A peaceful place in the middle of ugliness. Sandanti is the name of the woman who took me in. She's been really nice to me and has explained a lot. She explained my present situation and unknowingly resolved some questions about my past. My father and mother were both born here, but Mom left when I was an infant to protect me from an evil that was spreading here. I guess I can't blame her for that. I probably would have done the same if I were in her shoes. I miss her. I've been thinking about her a lot. I hope she is not worried about me. I hope she knows where to look for me when she realizes I'm missing. I hope

she already has. Anyway, I'm here now, and I am adapting to this strange place. And, today I made a new friend. Tarra is a wonderful little girl, and she's Sar's niece. So, that's it for now.

P.S. I'm glad I have you.

Sarah smiled, closed the book, and placed it next to Vente's dress, making sure to put the pencil in an outside pouch. She heard talking and laughing coming from the parlor. Just before she closed her bag, Sarah found a tiny mirror she had packed for emergencies. Mirrors were a versatile tool to have when stranded.

Sarah automatically went to look at her reflection but stopped before she flipped the mirror over. She remembered all the reflections she had seen of herself. After Tarra explained what they meant, she was fearful about what she might see. Sarah decided she had to know and slowly turned the mirror over.

At first, she was horrified by what she saw. Her hair was a disaster, and her skin was pale. The circles below her eyes were dark, and her eyes were glassy. Unlike the prior reflections, nothing else in the room around her had changed. That single observation made her look a little closer at her face. In that close inspection, she realized the veins that had been so visible in earlier views had become faint.

Almost instantaneously, Sarah put it together. *If the reflection shows what I really am inside, and my awful reflection is getting better, then maybe I'm on the right path after all. That's what they've been telling me. It's my journey.*

Sarah decided to keep the mirror in one of the outside pockets for easy access. If her theory was right, she would be able to judge her own progress with the mirror. For the first time since she arrived there, she did not feel lost. She wanted to have more control. It was like a compass.

Sarah had always been self-reliant in her old life, but since she arrived in the new one, she was forced to rely on others far more than she was used to. To that point, most seemed to have her best interests at heart, but Sarah remembered what her reflection looked like in the saloon after being in Arron's company for those few days. She made a solemn promise to never forget the anguish she felt that night, but she still remembered how good he made her feel.

Mentally shaking herself back into action, Sarah told herself she would probably have to combat those two separate issues at another time. Right then, all she wanted was to get into the parlor for Sandanti's story.

By the time everyone was comfortable in the parlor, it was nearly dusk. The sun was not shining through the windows anymore. It was a perfect setting to cozy up for a good story.

The children left the chair across from Sandanti unoccupied for Sarah. As she took her place in it, Tarra came up to her with a smile and sat down between Sarah's feet.

Sandanti steadied the fire and took a seat. She smiled at all the children, and after a moment of silence, she began her tale. It started with a young boy, and the fire in the parlor was high and bright. Her story ended with an old wise man, and the fire was only embers.

Peter was barely awake. Verd was sound asleep in front of the fire. Fara was sitting up with her arms around her knees, paying close attention to every detail of the story. Tarra had climbed up onto Sarah's lap somewhere between the wizard's battle and the witch's stew. She was still awake, but she was paying more attention to her blanket than to the story. Sarah was taking in the story and the wonderful warmth she felt from just being there.

When the story was over, Sandanti stood and motioned for Peter to take Verd to bed.

As the two boys left the room, Fara gave Sandanti a great hug and said, "That was wonderful! Thank you so very much."

Tarra sat up on Sarah's lap and said, "Will you tuck me in?"

Sarah looked at Sandanti for approval. Receiving it with no question, Sarah got up, held Tarra in the blanket, and brought her to bed.

"There you go." Sarah arranged the pillow and tucked the blanket in around Tarra's small body.

"Good night, Sarah." Tarra looked over the thick comforter.

"Good night, sweetie." Sarah backed out of the room, closing the door behind her.

She thought about going back out into the parlor to say good night to Sandanti, but she went to her room and quietly shut the door, taking care not wake the children.

Sarah took off her shirt, hung it over the bedpost, and folded her pants on the stool. She slipped into the sheets and let out a sigh. Although Sarah was unsure exactly what picking would entail, she was excited for it.

Sleep came easy to Sarah that night. When she got up, she stretched, brushed her hair and teeth, washed her face, got dressed, and joined the gang for breakfast.

The aroma was as wonderful as the day before. The only difference was that Sandanti was wearing a floor-length hiking dress and a brown apron.

Sarah noticed a small pile of baskets beside the front door. Once breakfast was served—and all mouths were full—she asked, "What is this picking anyway?"

A giggle swarmed over the table from the children.

Sandanti said, "Tomorrow, we leave for White Mountain, and we will need food for our journey. Today, we go pickin' the berries, fruits, and anything else the good Lord provides us."

Sarah nodded, but before she could feel too silly for asking, Sandanti said, "It would be nice if I could cook on the road, but since my mind is generally occupied with our safety, I prefer to bring along things that can be eaten as they are."

Sarah was happy for the explanation. She immediately thought of the pan and goblet in her bag and almost said something. She would wait and bring them out only if they were absolutely needed.

"Have all of you got your horses ready for our travels tomorrow?" Sandanti eyed each of the children suspiciously.

Sarah could tell the children still needed to tend to that very important chore.

Sandanti looked at Sarah and asked, "Do you have a horse of your own?"

Sarah remembered Spirit. "Well, there is this one horse

that I was able to ride from the stable in town, and the keeper said I could ride him whenever I wanted to."

Sandanti sat back in her chair and said, "You and I will have to get it prepared for the trip. Children, go tend to your mares while Sarah and I go get hers. When we return in a short while, we will be off."

A quick hustle of little legs ran past Sarah and out the front door.

Sandanti put some of the leftover bread away. "Just leave the dishes in the sink. We'll get them later."

As the two women left the house, Sarah remembered their first meeting. As they were walking back into town, she got very nervous. Her pace slowed, and her breathing became shallow. Before long, her face turned pale.

Sandanti did not notice anything amiss until she was walking alone. She stopped and looked back at the petrified young lady in the middle of the street. She walked back to Sarah and said, "It's okay. You do not need to fear this place—as long as you are sturdy in your own belief of good."

It took a second for that to get through Sarah's fear, but when it did, her shoulders relaxed and she was able to walk again. "What if he sees me?"

"The Dark Lord is not in the city now, yet he does have many spies. You will be seen, my child, and it will be reported. We will be well on our way to White Mountain before the news lands on his ears. Come now. The longer we stand here, the faster the news will catch up with us."

They made it into the stable with only a few folks noticing. Sarah did not feel very good about wandering in town, especially since she knew the news would get back to Arron. Once inside the stable, Sandanti followed Sarah to Spirit's stall.

Standing at the stall door, Sarah almost instantaneously felt relief. She wasn't sure why, but she had a special connection with the beautiful animal.

Sarah easily adorned Spirit with the harness and soft leather saddle.

The keeper came up behind them and said, "Ah, came back for her, didya? I thought perhaps she scared you off like the rest of 'em."

Sarah spun around. "No, sir. I was getting her ready to take her on a—"

Sandanti said, "Would you mind it if we took her out? We might not be back for a time."

Sticking his nose in the air in response to the lack of information, he said, "You can take this one forever for all I care. I could use the stall. Can't tame 'er, so she's no good to me."

"Is there a price?" Sandanti asked.

Rubbing his pointy, hairy chin, the small man said, "No, miss. No price." As he walked away, he mumbled, "Cost less than trying to sell 'er, and I'll make more money renting out the stall to a more mannered animal."

"Well then, child, I guess this one is all yours," Sandanti said.

Sarah didn't know what to think, but she felt on top of the world. All her life, she had wanted a horse of her own, but she had never had enough room or the means to care for one. Who would have thought her dream would come to pass in an unsuspecting place because of an unsuspecting little man? She ran her hand across Spirit's back and over her mane and said, "It's you and me then, I guess. If you don't mind?"

Sarah was not really expecting an answer, but Spirit turned her head toward Sarah and bowed. Sarah welcomed the answer.

Before the caretaker changed his mind, Sarah took Spirit by the reins—and the three of them made their way back to the house where the children were waiting.

℘ Chapter 11

BY THE TIME THEY WERE ON THEIR WAY, IT WAS BARELY midday, and the sun had not heated up the land to its hottest point. The breeze was a cool one, which helped keep the temperature comfortable.

The two boys and the oldest girl came up to Spirit.

"I've never seen another like her." Verd placed one hand on Spirit's neck and rubbed smoothly.

Fara looked at Sarah and said, "She's beautiful." She also caressed the soft hair on Spirit's neck.

Peter and Tarra stayed back by Sandanti, following the guidance of their caretaker. Sandanti had told them to wait until the others were done and not crowd the horse. The little ones were happy to oblige since Spirit was a giant to them.

When Verd and Fara were finished, Sandanti sent them in to grab the baskets. She ushered Peter and Tarra over to Spirit, looking at Sarah with the expectation that she would hold the reins tightly.

As the children approached, Spirit backed two steps away. With the loving touch of Sarah, Spirit stayed put so the children could come near.

Peter came over and touched Spirit's shoulder, which was the highest point he could reach. "She's big ... and soft."

Sarah chuckle and said, "Yes, she is, isn't she?"

Tarra's came over to say hello to the newest addition to their traveling party.

Peter backed away and stayed by Sarah's side.

Sarah said, "She won't hurt you, Tarra. Go ahead and pet her. I think she likes it."

Tarra took a step toward Spirit, placing herself in front of Sarah, and reached out to touch the huge horse. At first contact, Spirit moved, which startled Tarra and Sarah.

Sarah realized it was nothing and giggled while comforting Spirit and Tarra. She said, "Go ahead, Tarra."

Tarra took a deep breath and approached Spirit. She reached out her little hand and caressed Spirit's chin.

Spirit lowered her head a bit so the child could reach it better.

Tarra got swept away in the excitement and started to giggle. "She likes me!"

Just as she turned to give Sarah a big smile, Spirit turned and licked the top of Tarra's head, lifting all her hair over her face.

Tarra's smile turned into a look of disgust. "Gross."

Sarah and Sandanti both laughed, and Spirit seemed to think it was funny too, letting out a neigh of her own.

"Okay, introductions are over. It's time to be on our way." Sandanti fought to control her laughter.

Sarah walked Spirit over to the front deck and tied her reins to it. "I'll be right back." She would soon learn that Spirit was only unruly when she was around untrustworthy people. For the most part, she was quite a loving creature. She did have a very strong spirit, which was the source of her name.

Sarah went into her room and grabbed her bag. She thought they would be coming back, but since she could never really be sure what was going to happen, she thought it would be wise to have her possessions with her on the journey.

The children waited quietly at the edge of the porch while Sandanti finished locking up. When she was ready, they went to the small stable and collected their ponies and horses.

Sandanti's horse was old but muscular. Its white-and-black spotted coat was in stark contrast to its dark brown mane.

Sarah mounted Spirit, and they made a straight line toward the prairie. She hadn't seen an end to it from the house, and she was increasingly impressed by its size and beauty.

They traveled in single file or with Verd in the lead. Peter, Fara, and Sandanti followed. Tarra rode with Sandanti since she was too small to ride her own horse. Sarah took up the back.

They rode for a long while before they could see a heavily wooded area in the distance.

"Almost there," Sandanti said.

The children shouted with glee.

Sarah didn't blame them for being a little impatient. It was an awfully long ride, she thought, for picking berries. Perhaps she had just been spoiled in her world with convenience stores and supermarkets.

When they arrived at the edge of the woods, Sarah was delighted by the shade. The brush added to the coolness of the air.

They got off the horses and started off with their bags. Peter suggested a contest to see who could pick the most berries. Sandanti stayed behind with the horses.

Sarah and Tarra went to look for their own bushel of berries. The two of them were having so much fun. Sarah loved it when Tarra insisted that she be picked up to reach a particular berry. Sarah happily obliged every time. Their bags and baskets were getting heavy, and their mouths and fingers were sticky from snacking on their find.

Sarah was kneeling down to wipe a piece of berry from Tarra's face when Tarra bit down on a berry and squirted juice onto Sarah's cheek. The two of them burst into laughter, and Sarah began to chase Tarra around the bushes and across the paths that wound through the trees. Around one turn and then another, Sarah was giggling and running so much that she thought her sides would split. No feeling could have been better for her right then. She was having the time of her life.

Then before another laugh could be spouted or another breath taken, Tarra was scooped by Arron. Sarah looked up into his eyes. Fear overwhelmed her senses. She knew right then that Arron was the Dark Lord she had been warned about.

Tarra stopped laughing and looked down at Sarah.

"Put her down," Sarah said quietly.

"Oh, but I believe she belongs to me, my lady," he replied with an evil look in his eye. Sarah wondered if that look had been there all along. If so, how could she have missed it?

"She belongs to no one but herself," Sarah said with a little less fear in her voice. She physically felt the fear in her limbs.

"Sarah!" Tarra shouted as Arron started to turn away, still holding her tightly.

"Wait!" Sarah yelled. "It's not her you want—it's me. Let her go!"

Arron stopped and said, "That is very noble of you, but I don't think you really understand yet who you are. This little one already knows who she is. For me, that is a bigger threat than your blundering soul."

Sarah stood completely still, not knowing what to do next. She saw the fear on Tarra's face and wished she had some magic to get her out of his grip.

"Please let her be! She's just a little girl." Sarah tried not to sound demanding.

"And watch her and her power grow to be used against me? I think not." He chuckled evilly.

Tarra struggled to get free, and the Dark Lord said, "If you want her, you will have to come get her yourself—and I highly doubt you have the stomach for that."

His horse raised both front legs, and with a shrieking yelp from the little girl, the Dark Lord took off at lightning speed.

Sarah ran back to Sandanti and told her what had happened. Sandanti was panicked, but the other children were still in the forest. She could not leave them vulnerable to another attack.

"What should we do?" Sarah asked.

"I need to collect the others. You need to go after Tarra!" Sandanti quickly packed up the horses. She grabbed Sarah and said, "You have been here long enough, and I have explained enough to you. You know in your heart who you are, and you know in your heart what you have to do."

Sarah understood, and the clarity showed in her eyes.

Sandanti said, "Go do it!" She left with the remaining horses to go find the other children.

Sarah took out her mirror and thought about the chase ahead. Her reflection was clearer than before. It was what she was meant to do. She knew it. Without another moment's hesitation, Sarah got onto Spirit's back. She whispered in Spirit's ear, and they took off like lightning. Spirit understood the urgency of their plight and spread her wings. They were on the hunt for Tarra and the Dark Lord.

Spirit used the currents to navigate through the air, and Sarah's eyes focused on the land below. They flew for several minutes but did not see them anywhere. "Where are they?" she shouted into the wind. Sarah looked around intently. Her eyes became sharp, and she could make out tiny details on the ground. She would notice the difference in her vision later. She had good eyesight before, but it had become perfect vision for almost any condition.

When Sarah finally spotted them, they were riding in and out of the tree line. The speed of Arron's horse was unprecedented. Tarra was holding on for dear life. Arron had her in front of him and was covering her far too well for Sarah to get a good look.

The Dark City was approaching fast, and soldiers in the towers were watching the skies. They hadn't spotted her yet—and she didn't want them to. It was her only edge at that point.

Spirit began to descend. Sarah held on to her mane like she had been riding her for years. When they got closer to the ground, Sarah tightened her grip. Spirit's stride was not broken in the least. Her hooves hit the ground running with the same speed and endurance, and Sarah was impressed and honored to be on Spirit's back.

Sarah's knew she would probably become Arron's prisoner too. She slowed Spirit down and unhappily pulled her into the forest.

Coming to a stop, Sarah saw Arron charging toward the front gate of the Dark City. She had entered through that gate willingly—not too long ago. She already felt like a different person than she was then.

Sarah put her head down onto Spirit's mane and took a moment to think. She decided that the best course of action would be to get to the White Mountain of Eslinar. She didn't know what was there, but she knew it was Taurik, Sar, and Sandanti's destination. With a kick to Spirit's side, she said, "Let's go!" And they took off the way they came.

They covered much distance on the ground before the terrain became increasingly treacherous. The ground was either too steep or rocky, covered by swamp, or blanketed in a thick forest. It was almost impassible in spots. Sarah slowed Spirit to a walk and decided they would be faster and have better luck in the air. She was confident they were far enough from the Dark City that being spotted was no longer an issue.

She backed Spirit up a quarter mile to pick up enough speed and started her running. It was only a matter of moments before they were soaring through the air. They flew over the obstacles that threatened to halt their journey. From up there, the inhospitable land looked marvelous. Hills and valleys were covered in impenetrable brush, and a winding river cut its way through it like a knife through butter.

Sarah wanted to go down to investigate but decided to go back when it was all over. Her goal was to get to White Mountain. She knew she would find help there.

Sarah took Spirit back up to their previous height and turned her focus to White Mountain. They had a breathtaking panoramic view of the area. The mountain stretched into the clouds, and its peaks were covered in a blanket of snow and ice. The smooth rocks that made up the faces of its cliffs were beautiful, bright, and white. The sides of the mountain were green, red, orange, and blue. Sarah thought it would make a wonderful picture. She had never seen such beauty in one place. What a story she could tell. No one would believe her.

Sarah's attention was diverted from the boundless beauty of the mountain to what peeked out from the far side. Slowly—and with much power and grandeur—Eslinar emerged. The tower was built up against the side of the tallest mountain, and pieces were built out in every direction.

The rock came from the mountain and served as camouflage. It also looked to be a highly effective watchtower. Sarah knew she was approaching unannounced and decided to keep a close watch on the towers. She did not want to be surprised by anything that might come out of them.

The columns of rock and mortar grew out from the mountain, and the peaks and valleys matched the intensity of the mountain formation itself. Long, narrow slits at even intervals spanned the entire length of the city. The structure seemed to go on for miles. As she would find out later, it truly did. Parts of the enormous city couldn't be seen from anywhere outside of the walls.

Sarah decided they needed to get back on the ground. She pushed Spirit to go a little farther—and she was glad she did.

A massive waterfall with ice-blue water fell seamlessly over the top of the farthest peak. All around its life-giving flow, thick greens of all varieties grew. Much like the rest of the scenery, it was speckled with beautiful reds and blues. There was gold around the banks of the waterfall.

They landed a hundred yards or so from the falls. The sound was overwhelmingly loud and soft at the same time. Sarah dismounted, and Spirit began to graze. Sarah stood and took in the scenery. She had been searching for something or someplace this beautiful for her whole career. Now that her career didn't matter to her anymore, she had found it.

She took a deep breath of the wonderfully pure air and looked for any signs of habitation. She didn't want to forget that she was unannounced.

Not too far beyond the tree line, Sarah saw a rooftop. As she approached, she saw that it was dilapidated. It was on top of a small house that was not in much better condition.

The wooden house stood out as an oddity in a place of such beauty. She carefully made her way closer to the door while looking around. She did not want to be caught by surprise. She knew she was going to have to make herself known, if she was not already, to the people there. Tarra needed her, and she was going to do anything to get to her.

Sarah knew the Dark Lord's powers went well beyond the things she could see with her eyes. Her senses had been overwhelmed a number of times in his presence. If Tarra stayed with the Dark Lord long enough, he might deplete her unique sensibilities—and then she would not want to leave. Sarah could not bear to think of that. She decided to use the small house as a home base. She took a look around and found nothing but a table, some chairs, lots of dust, and a dirty window.

I guess this will do.

From outside, Sarah heard a shuffling in the leaves. She leaned against the wall next to the front entrance. She knew someone was outside, and from the staggered shuffling, Sarah could tell there were more than one of them. She shuddered.

They moved quietly to the opening of the door.

Sarah remained perfectly still, but her breath was hard. The handle on the bottom half of the two-part door started to turn. They were coming in. Sarah got ready for a fight. Her chest was heavy with air. She knew she had come too far to have it end there. The door opened, and before the figure could make it in all the way, Sarah pounced.

Sarah got a couple of good shots in, but the fury was taken out of her fight when she heard a chuckle coming from the front door. She stopped swinging—and so did the figure she had been sparring with.

"Well, well, well. You certainly have gained a bit more bite in that bark of yours through your travels," Taurik said.

ᘔ Chapter 12

Sarah smiled, breathed a great sigh of relief, and ran into his arms. They hugged for a minute and laughed, and then she remembered the figure she had been sparring with.

Sar was a bit ruffled, but he was grinning from ear to ear.

"Oh, Sar!" She gasped, hugged him, and looked him over for anything she might have done to him. Remembering he was a warrior, she brushed off his shoulder like she was getting a piece of lint off a suit.

He smiled a big, jagged-tooth smile, and the three of them laughed together.

Taurik said, "We have been trying to track you, Sarah, but I lost you at the Dark City. I cannot enter unnoticed. What happened?" He brushed the hair from her face.

Sarah passed them in the doorway and walked out near the waterfall. "It's hard to say really. I thought I … I thought I knew myself. But the mirrors and Sandanti and …" Sarah spun around and yelped. "Tarra! We have to get Tarra out of there. The Dark Lord took her from me, and he took her to his city. I rode Spirit here to get help and get her out. I feel stronger than ever before, but I know better than to think I can do this alone."

Sar and Taurik exchanged nods.

"We will get her," Sar said. "Rushing will not aid our effort—let us eat."

The three of them cleared a patch of dried wood to the side of the house and brought the timber inside to the stove. Sarah began to dust off the furniture, and Taurik went back to the main castle to raid the kitchen for goods he could bring back to the cabin without upsetting the cook or his staff.

When Taurik returned, Sarah and Sar were waiting on the porch and admiring the simple tranquility of the location.

"Hungry?" Taurik shouted as he came up the path that connected the cabin to the rest of the grounds. He was holding a bundle of fruit and a huge slab of meat.

"Not sure I'm that hungry," Sarah said and chuckled.

"Not all for you." Sar got up to take the beef from Taurik.

The three of them retired inside to prepare the meal. Sar did most of the preparing, and Taurik started a fire in the small fireplace.

Sarah got the table ready with silverware. *Not too fancy, but it will certainly do.*

The cabin took on a wonderful aroma just as the sun started to set. The combination of smells, shadows on the walls, and crackling of the fire caused Sarah to almost fall asleep where she sat.

Sar cut the meat and put it on the plates. "Eat," he said without bothering to look up. He was probably too hungry—and the meat smelled far too good—to concentrate on the human idea of politeness.

Taurik joined Sar and Sarah at the table, and they dug into the food.

Sarah couldn't help but notice that Sar's portion was three or four times the size of hers. "You're really going to eat all of that?"

It did not take very long for her to have her answer.

Sar did not say a word, but within minutes, he was wiping his chin on his sleeve and belching loudly. He looked at Sarah, grinned, and said, "Excuse me."

After the food was gone—and their stomachs were satisfied—they cleared the table.

Sarah leaned in and asked, "What's the plan now? What are we supposed to do about Tarra? We can't wait too long. Every second she is with him makes her more vulnerable to giving in to the dark side of herself. If we wait too long, she might not come back to us at all."

Taurik and Sar exchanged a glance. Taurik stood, moved over to the fireplace, and said, "Unfortunately, it's not up to us whether Tarra holds onto the dark or the light. She has a choice, and it is not ours to make."

"But she's just a child!" Sarah exclaimed.

Taurik said, "Yes, she is a child. In the other world that you knew as a child, the same battle had to be won in each and every being. Some went to the dark side, but most stayed to the light. However, in that world, you cannot see the inner battle one might be fighting—and you certainly cannot check their progress without speaking. In this world, inner decisions are tangible. Once you decide which way to go, you become your decision—for all to see. We will help you retrieve Tarra. We know she was on her way to join the White City. We do not believe any beings should be forced to change their decisions once they have been made. However, if we do succeed, you must know that she might not want to leave. Furthermore, she might even help the Dark Lord fight us off."

"If what you're telling me is true, there is no way to know unless we try. I can't just leave her there—and I won't!" Sarah did not like the sound of what Taurik was saying, and the more he spoke, the more she felt like they were wasting time by sitting there. "We need to act now. I don't understand. We've eaten and rested—why we are still sitting here. We should be getting the army together or something." She hoped they hadn't waited too long already.

Taurik looked at Sar and Sarah with concern and frustration. "You still think like one from the other world. Do you truly think that moving against the Dark City with ambition and pride alone will get Tarra back?"

"Is there another way?" Sarah asked.

Taurik said, "We cannot charge the city and expect victory. The Dark Lord knows that. Even with our mercenaries under my charge, his army numbers us twenty to one at best, and they would destroy us in combat within a day."

"If what you're trying to tell me is true, why hasn't he taken over this city?" Sarah stood and swung her arms. "Why hasn't he taken Eslinar for his own? I find it hard to believe much of anything I've heard so far. And if it weren't for my own change since I came here, I would think you were full of shit." Sarah walked over to the door and stared out at the waterfall. She took a deep breath and listened to the rush of the water.

She had been so happy to see the pair and get help. There was another reason she was happy to see Taurik, but she stuffed that thought away. She was too angry to consider that possibility.

After a few minutes, Sar said, "I see your temper hasn't changed much. What you did not let him say was the elders of Eslinar charge the regular army—not him."

Taurik snickered.

Sarah spun around to give him a piece of her mind, but she remembered where her last outburst with these two had led her. She held her tongue long enough to look into Taurik's eyes and see that he was not trying to be difficult. He was telling the truth. She came back to the table and sat down.

Taurik put more wood in the fire to help light the room.

"Okay. Perhaps I still have a long way to go in the temper department," Sarah said with a grin.

Sar returned the grin with a wide smile and a contagious laugh.

The trio chuckled until the tension was completely gone.

Sar got up from the table and put together three cups of something that tasted like tea. "It's powerful." He put the cups down on the table.

Taking a sip of the liquid, Sarah winced. She would certainly take Sar's word for it and sipped a little. "Okay. If we can't charge the city and take Tarra back by force, what can we do?"

"You have met Sandanti?" Taurik asked.

"Yes, she told me a lot and helped me understand some of this." Sarah felt sad. Sandanti had given her so much information and a lot of care, but the day with Tarra had made Sarah understand the most about herself. She didn't know if it was a good time to say anything. She shook off the thought before the dread for Tarra's well-being overwhelmed her again.

"She is very powerful and will be an essential part of this if we are to get Tarra back in one piece."

"I just left Sandanti before I made it here. I left her in the woods with the other children."

"Sit, Sarah. They are fine. Word has come to us that they will be arriving here in the next two nights. We will watch for them. We will not act, however, until she arrives."

"That long?" Sarah felt her anger rising again.

"She is one of our elders and must be here when the council meets. We will then—and only then—decide the course. It has become apparent, since your arrival here in this world, that the time has come to make a stand. We must take back the souls stolen by darkness."

Sarah said, "How did getting Tarra back turn into making a stand?" She chuckled and leaned back in her seat. "And you two tell me that I'm dramatic."

Sar sat with a blank face and sipped his cup.

Taurik said, "This is about you, Sarah. Our people have been waiting for you to come. You are the key, the one, the only soul who can help us destroy the evil in our lands forever."

"No pressure," Sarah said sarcastically. "Oh, come on. That was a little funny." She looked back and forth between the two.

Still nothing.

"It's your council, Sarah," Taurik said. "The White

City has been awaiting your arrival for my whole life. I was raised knowing of you. I am sorry you cannot say the same." He seemed saddened by the thought. "You may not understand, but in time, you will. You will come to know that I have not said anything to you in undo fairness because you needed to find your own way. I did not want—and neither did anyone else—to lead you down the road that was not meant to be yours by filling your mind with facts you were not ready for. You had to learn the way you did—or else we would not be here now." Taurik took the last sip of his cup, nodded at Sar, and excused himself from the room.

Sarah had never seen Taurik in such a state.

"He cares for you much," Sar said. "He is only telling you the truth as he sees you can handle it. And so far, Miss Sarah, your words tell me that you cannot. Although you do look much better than when your temper had you leave us in the forest."

Sarah sat back and took a deep breath. She combed her hair back with her fingers and said, "You're right."

Sar got up to go outside.

Sarah said, "No, I'll go." She got up from her chair and softly passed Sar in the doorway. She went out to look for Taurik.

Taurik had made his way to the lake and sat on a small boulder by the rolling water.

Sarah approached him and said, "Two days then?" She knew that his disbelief was deserved. "You haven't led me wrong yet." She joined him on the boulder. "Besides, you say this council is mine, and I am very curious to hear what they have to say." She stood up, giggled, and pulled on his hand. "And you, Sir Taurik, are officially requested to take me, Sarah—the chosen one—on the grand tour of this beautiful castle."

Taurik smiled and took her hand.

They went back to the cabin to clean up and collect Sarah's limited belongings. Sarah, Taurik, and Sar returned to the castle.

The path was long and overflowing with beautiful flowers and perfectly sculpted shrubbery. The trees were blowing peacefully in the breeze, and the softness of it all hit Sarah's face. For a moment, she was at peace. She could feel the tranquility of the purples, greens, and whites that surrounded the path.

When they reached an opening in the brush, Sarah was disappointed. The feeling was quickly replaced with excitement about the overwhelming beauty of the castle. From where they stood, Sarah could see the gates. From the air, she could see them—but not in so much detail. The stone doorway seemed a hundred feet tall and was adorned with the hand-carved art of many men over many thousands of years.

As they got closer, Sarah could make out pictures of men in battle armor, archers and chariots, kings and queens, monsters and demons being slain, and people rejoicing and feasting. It was not just art; it was history.

The outer walls were lined with the same beautiful foliage as the path. The contrast of the colors of thousands of flowers against the stark white-gray marble of the stone walls was breathtaking. Sarah remembered walking into the Dark Lord's city, and she knew she was in the right place. She was surrounded by a warm blanket of comfort and home.

Walking through the massive archway, a whole world was revealed to Sarah. It was full of beauty and peace. The beautiful buildings were small, but they were built in fluidity with the white stone of the perimeter. Inside, finely crafted wood intertwined with the stone. It had all been put together with care, and every detail was perfect. Lanterns of the finest metals hung inside and outside all the houses and shops.

When the trio entered, the people who were walking about kept moving, but it didn't take long for all the movement to stop. The people became eerily quiet, and one group after another went to their knees and bowed to them.

Sarah whispered, "Taurik, who are they bowing to?"

"You."

After all she had seen, learned, and experienced since she arrived in that world, she probably should have expected that. Instead, Sarah was taken aback. She fought back tears of absolute joy. She knew for the first time in her life that she had a purpose. Although she still did not know what exactly that purpose was, she knew it was there—and she would find it. Sarah could feel nothing but happiness to be alive.

When they arrived at the main building, Taurik put his fist to his chest in an honorable gesture to Sar. Sar returned the salute, looked at Sara, and smiled. He then turned and left them.

Taurik and Sarah entered through the smaller archway into the main hallway. It was elegant and lit by large lanterns that were evenly spaced for as far as Sarah could see. The carved windows were perfectly symmetrical.

Taurik was glowing. He tapped Sarah on the shoulder, pointed, whispered, "Sarah, look."

Sarah looked down the hallway, and her heart fell in happiness, confusion, and awe. "Mom!" She ran to her mother with arms stretched out like a child.

After a long embrace, Gratt—who was known as Grattiella in that world—took Sarah by the face with a gentle grasp and said, "Come." She led Sarah to her room, which was more like a small estate.

"Mom, what is this place?"

"This is your true home." Grattiella watched her daughter walk slowly into the foyer. "Quite different from what you're used to, I know. This was to have been your room had I been able to raise you here."

Sarah looked back at her mother with a twinkle in her eye. She had been through so much there already, but seeing her mother made her remember in detail the one-bedroom apartment Grattiella had struggled to keep. Thinking back to the warm dinners and the love that filled that small pad of theirs, Sarah smiled. It was small, but it was home. Her thoughts returned to where she was; it was grand, but it still had a warm, loving feel to every inch. Sarah realized that her mother looked grand too.

When she had said good-bye to her before her vacation, she had left her mother in the garden in front of the small bungalow she had purchased for her retirement. She had been wearing ripped jeans, a worn denim shirt, and a straw hat that protected her hair from the sun.

The same woman stood before her with a long braid, and flowers elegantly decorated her beautiful red hair, which was speckled with gray. She wore a black velvet dress that had intricate purple and gold embroidery. The sleeves of the fine-quality dress came down over her hands, gracefully revealing a large ruby ring.

When her mother turned, Sarah saw that the back of the dress was perfectly aligned with her shape. It flowed seamlessly to the floor, and only a whisper of material touched as she walked.

Sarah was impressed, and she wondered why she had never noticed her mother's nobility prior to that moment.

Sarah had been in this new world long enough to see strange things, make strange friends, find her inner self, and grow stronger than she had ever been. However, in that moment, she felt like a little girl again. She walked over to her mother and gave her a very long hug.

≈ Chapter 13

GRATTIELLA GUIDED SARAH THROUGH THE REST OF THE castle.

As they walked back to her quarters, Sarah said, "Why didn't you tell me of this place? Did you think I wouldn't believe you?"

"Oh, but I did," Grattiella replied calmly with a smile at the corner of her lips. Taking Sarah's hand, she continued, "Don't you remember the stories I would tell you at bedtime when you were a child?"

Sarah looked puzzled and then her eyes lit up. "The fairy tales?" She gasped.

"The fairytales." Grattiella nodded.

Sarah started to laugh, and before she knew it, she was engulfed in a full-blown laughing fit. "I ... just ... thought ... you ... had a ... really big ... imagination." When she caught her breath, she said, "Those stories weren't fairy tales?"

"They were more like history lessons," Grattiella replied as they went through another doorway. "This is yours," Grattiella said as they entered a suite on the eastern corner of the castle.

Looking around, Sarah was inwardly at peace. It was a beautiful room. Although back where she grew up, it would have been referred to as a wing.

"This was meant for you when you were born to us," Grattiella said.

"And it was kept for me all this time?" Sarah imagined a lifetime of keeping a room like a shrine.

"They would have kept your home intact for as long as it took." Grattiella crossed over to the window and looked out over the land. "I did miss it here." She took a deep breath of the cool, wet air, stepped back, and turned to Sarah. "I am sorry you didn't get to grow up here."

Sarah pulled out a white linen item of clothing from the beautifully carved armoire. "Is this for me?" Sarah asked, admiring the delicate strength of the material.

"Everything here is for you, Sarah. Why don't we get you cleaned up?" She took the linen from Sarah and brought her to the bath that had been drawn for her.

Sarah's clothes were tattered, dirty, and worn. She had put them through a lot. She realized how badly a bath was needed; it had been far too long since her last one. She did not feel badly about that since the circumstances of her adventure had not exactly given her the opportunity. She slid into the perfume-scented water and relaxed her muscles.

She thought of all the tales her mother had told her growing up and saw them in a new light. The warmth of the water soothed her body. Her mind relaxed a bit, but it was working hard at putting together the facts as she knew them. She had enough information to understand what was going on, where she was, and why she was there. There was a comfort in knowing that bigger things were always at work in her life.

She stepped out of the bath and dried off. A couple of her wounds needed to be dressed by the servants who came in with her towels. After they left, Sarah went over to the wardrobe and took out the fabric she had been holding before.

Grattiella came back into the room and said, "Here, let me." She took the fabric from Sarah and lovingly showed her how it wrapped around her torso. She took out a roll of golden yarn and wrapped that around her too. When she was finished, Sarah looked into the standing mirror and saw that it was even more beautiful than when she held it.

The white linen was woven from the finest thread. It hung loose on her shoulders and was tight around her chest. The golden yarn crisscrossed her bosom and held the fabric in place better than anything she had ever seen. It was beautiful. Below her waist, it fell loosely to just above her knees.

Grattiella caught the look in Sarah's eyes, chuckled, and handed her a bundle of soft brown leather.

Sarah smiled and slipped on the leather boots. They fit perfectly. Coming halfway up her leg, the leather was light in weight and in color, and it was amazingly comfortable.

Grattiella guided Sarah to a wooden bench near the mirror. The servant woman began to put on the leather boots. It took a few minutes to lace them up.

While the soft boots were being laced, Grattiella braided Sarah's hair. When she was done, Grattiella said, "Now you are now dressed as you should be—as you would have been all along."

Sarah looked in the mirror and couldn't believe what she saw. She did not see the awkward young lady who would stand behind a camera and take pictures of others. She saw a …

"Warrior," Grattiella said with a loving hand on her daughter's shoulder.

"A beautiful one at that," Taurik said from the doorway.

"Taurik, it's so good of you to come as I asked." Grattiella waved for him to enter.

The servants departed with the towels and Sarah's worn clothes.

Sarah and Taurik shared a moment's glance. With a smile and a blush of her cheek, Sarah turned toward the window.

Taurik walked directly to her and kissed her hand. "May I introduce myself?"

Sarah giggled. "But I know you already, Taurik."

"Do you?" He smirked and took a few steps back.

Grattiella took one hand of each of them and walked them over to the window. She stood between them as they looked out over the land.

Sarah was waiting for someone to fill her in, but she was not anxious. She waited easily and without haste. Her vision was filled with some of the most breathtaking views she had ever seen—and she had her mother again.

"Sarah," Grattiella said softly, "Taurik was meant to be your husband. He was raised knowing of you. He is your prince."

Sarah started laughing.

Taurik looked at Grattiella with concern, but both of them were too stunned by her reaction to say anything.

"It wasn't all that long ago, Mom, that I was living in a small home—working every day—with nothing but the passion in my heart. I was even hungry most days."

Grattiella looked stunned. "Why didn't you come?"

"I didn't want you to worry more than I already knew you did. I got by. I decided to give myself a well-deserved break, and the weather turned on me. I rested under some trees and found myself here in this world. I am a princess here, and I live in a magnificent palace. I am dressed in fine linen—and now you tell me that a heroic, handsome prince is to be my husband. It's just too perfect. It's a dream." She sat on the finely embroidered chair near the bed. "Is this real? Was my past real?"

Grattiella knelt at Sarah's feet and said, "Both are real. Your past was as real as your present, and if it were not for your past, you would not have your present. This, right here and now, is what you were meant to be—how you were meant to live."

Sarah looked into her mother's eyes and saw concern and love. "I'm glad you're here with me."

While Sarah and Grattiella hugged, Taurik remained by the window and tried to understand what Sarah was going through. However, he could not. He had always known of her and of the other world. He could not imagine how disorienting the whole experience must have been for her. His concern turned to sadness, and he turned away. He knew he would be with her, but it would have to be in her time.

Sarah walked over to Taurik and took his hand. "It's just all so much to take in. I never knew my childhood stories were facts. I thought they were just fairy tales told to children to let them know that life can be good. It's just a lot to take in."

"I understand, Sarah," Taurik said in a gentle voice. "I should go." He turned to leave, but Sarah tightened her grip on his hand.

"No, don't." Her eyes filled with contentment. "I don't want you to leave."

"You don't?" he asked.

"No. Please stay. You have been so good to me. You have protected me and comforted me—and you even tried to talk some sense into me."

They looked to each other with compassion and understanding.

"Mother, would be so kind as to give us a moment?" she asked without taking her eyes off Taurik.

Grattiella departed with a small smile.

Once the door was closed, Sarah looked intently at Taurik and said, "I would be happy to be your bride."

Taurik's smile grew, and he grabbed Sarah by the waist, swinging her around.

They both laughed.

Sarah took Taurik over to the sitting area and looked him square in the eyes. "But first, will you help me?"

"Of course," Taurik replied with a schoolboy's smile "What is it you need?"

"Tarra," she said, shifting the mood in the room.

Taurik sat down and took a deep breath. "Sarah, are you sure you want to do this now? She has most likely been lost to us."

"Most likely isn't a good enough reason not to try. And yes now. Today! We can't wait much longer." She walked quickly to the window. "The longer we wait, the further down that thing's slippery slope she falls. She is strong, but she is a child. We must try!"

Taurik joined her at the window and took her hand. "Then we try." He smiled and said, "But first we eat."

"Eat?"

"Yes," Taurik replied. "We won't get very far if we are starving, will we?"

Sarah knew he had a good point. She took his arm, and they walked to the dining room.

Sandanti and many others were waiting for them.

Sarah was ushered to a seat to the right of the head of the table. Food of the finest kind was served in the most elegant way Sarah had ever encountered. She looked to the empty seat and wondered who would sit there.

Grattiella reached over the table and said, "You will meet him soon, my dear."

"Meet who?" The idea of meeting another person of obvious significance excited Sarah. She did not know if she could emotionally handle another right then.

Three servants escorted an old man to the head of the table. One pulled out his chair, another took his ornate cape from around his neck, and the third poured his wine.

"An old friend of your father," Grattiella said quietly as the servants left. "Rika is his given name."

After the stout man was settled, he stroked his long, white beard and looked at his guests. His eyes met Sarah's, and he sat back with a lighthearted twinkle in his eyes. "Ah, so you have joined us. I had been told you were here. Are you well, my child?"

Sarah was amazed by the old man's grace. He seemed wise and concerned about her.

"I am well. Thank you." She looked down at her empty plate.

The old man signaled for the servants to begin serving the main course, and as the attendees became distracted, he touched her chin and pulled her face up to meet his. "Child," he whispered, "do not be concerned with what I may think of you. It is what you think of yourself that holds the heaviest weight." He winked and called for his goblet to be refilled.

The food was perfect, and Sarah had not realized how hungry she was. She tried not to shovel her food but was unsuccessful. Her mother looked at her with a smile and motioned for Sarah to wipe the glop of potatoes from the side of her lip.

After many mouthfuls, Sarah reached for her goblet and took a sip. She felt refreshed and content. Her blood grew warmer, her stomach began to feel full, and her head became light. Even her vision blurred. A look of fear passed over her face as she tried to push off the sensation. She put down the goblet, and the flashes grew stronger. She could see Tarra in a dark room. Her face was dirty, her hands were bloody, and she was being teased with a drink. Tarra cried out.

Sarah stood, hit the wall behind her seat, and she too cried out.

Taurik caught her fall, and Grattiella reached out for her.

After a moment, Sarah came back. Her breast heaved with dread and sadness. She looked at Taurik and said, "We leave now."

Without hesitation, Taurik motioned to Sar, Sandanti, and Tinbe.

Sarah quickly left the dining hall. "We must leave now. She is in danger and is being treated badly. The bastard. Gather the militia, Taurik. By that time, I will be ready. I will meet with you on the back fields. Tinbe, Sar, go with Taurik. Help him gather all the muscle you can."

"I will sound the alarm." Taurik started to motion for his general.

Sarah stopped in her tracks and said, "No. No alarm. The element of surprise will be ours as long as the fates will allow us to have it. Sandanti, follow me."

Taurik took the men and began gathering the militia.

By the time Sandanti and Sarah reached Sarah's suite, Sandanti was winded.

"Help me." Sarah swung open the doors to the wardrobe and threw three pieces of clothing on the bed. She knew they were for war.

"You move with much haste, child." Sandanti helped Sarah tie the straps of the leather armor.

Sarah finished tying her boots and stood tall. "I have never been more sure of what I had to do than this very minute. You had faith in me once—have faith in me now." She took off past her mother without another word.

Grattiella and Sandanti looked at each other and nodded. Grattiella said, "It's time." The two of them left to go meet with Rika, and Taurik returned to Sarah.

"Show me to the stable," Sarah said. "Please."

The stable had room for at least a hundred horses and the finest accommodations for its tenants. Taurik took Sarah straight to Spirit.

Spirit's mane had been combed, her coat had been washed, and she had been adorned with a beautifully marked saddle.

"Made for a princess," Taurik said as he watched Sarah examining the decorations.

Sarah nodded and touched Spirit's neck. She glided her hand along Spirit's smooth skin. She walked slowly around the horse and placed her head on Spirit's brow.

After a few minutes, Sarah raised her head and began taking off the ornate decorations, leaving only a woven blanket on her back.

Taurik said, "What are you doing?"

Sarah mounted Spirit and guided her out of the stall. "Her name is all she needs."

Two legends had been united.

Taurik nodded and mounted his own steed. They rode out to the field where the men, women, and beasts were gathered to join Sarah in her fight.

When they exited the southwestern gate, Sarah said, "This is your militia?"

Hundreds of warrior men and women held shields, swords, and spears. They were dressed in battle gear, and many rode horses. Sarah noticed a robust beast with a light blue complexion and stark white hair that draped over his chest. He wore the same woven leather armor as the other warriors. When they passed him, he followed.

Taurik and Sarah stopped about three hundred feet in front of the line. The masses began to quiet, and she scanned the faces of the warriors.

The lower ranks wore little armor, but they had painted their bodies with intricate war patterns. Every soul she could see—with all skin tones, hair colors, and types of shields—was ready and looking right at her.

She turned Spirit to face the small group that had formed behind her and rode to meet with them. "There are so many," Sarah said to Taurik and Sar.

"Not nearly as many as we should need." Taurik replied.

"Plan you do have, Miss Sarah, yes?" Tinbe asked.

Sarah turned at the sound of his voice. She was pleased with those who would be leading with her. She looked at Tinbe and the others and realized she had not thought of the repercussions of moving forward without a plan. Should she tell them? Should she lead them to believe she actually knew what she was doing because of some divine providence they were convinced she had?

She took a moment to let it sink in that their fates were in her hands. They might all die that day if she gave the order to attack the Dark City, but they all probably knew that all ready. They still chose to stand behind her.

Spirit shuffled underneath as Sarah's vision blurred again. For a moment, she could only see Tarra. She was frightened but unwavering, and she was calling to Sarah for help.

When Sarah could see again, she ran a circle around the men, waiting for the answer to Tinbe's important question. "The plan I have is not complete without the aid of you fine men. I need time and cover. I need to get to Tarra. I can see her in my mind, and from my memory of the Dark City, I know where to find her. I need you and your men to give me time—a distraction—to keep the Dark Lord and his men busy long enough for me to get to her."

Sar said, "And when you find her?"

Sarah sat back and let the reins loosen. If she was going to be honest with the men, it was time. "I don't know. I'm not certain about the outcome. I'm not even certain that what I am doing is the right thing. What I do know for sure is that everything in my being is telling me to go this way. To do this. To find her. Somehow I just know that when I do, it will all be right."

They knew the truth. She was not, in her own mind, being led by some divine providence. It was more of a gut feeling. From the shifting and glancing, Sarah could tell it was not what they had expected to hear.

After a few moments, Taurik said, "We have all known—even before Sarah did—that she was the one. We have watched her grow and make use of one of the skills the Great One has bestowed upon her. We had faith in her long before she did. She is listening to the very part of her we have been ushering her to all this while. I say we give her the time she needs. I say we fight. All that are with us be with us."

Sarah nodded to Taurik and said, "And all those who choose not to be may go without any dishonor in my eyes or the eyes of any other."

Sar hit his chest plate and said, "My allegiance is with you. We go."

The rest of the circle grinned and nodded to Sarah.

She smiled and ran a circle around her men.

They followed her out of the circle and screamed their battle cries.

∂ Chapter 14

THE MASS OF ARMORED, WEAPON-WIELDING WARRIORS
followed the war cry, and they took off toward the
Dark City with a fury never before seen in that land.

Sarah and Spirit ran alongside their brothers-in-arms,
and Spirit's hooves parted from the land. When Spirit lifted
them above the treetops, Sarah heard the roar of the many
who followed and felt strong.

After a time, the sound of her soldiers grew quieter.
When she no longer heard them, she looked back and saw
they were walking. Spirit turned, and they flew over the
mass, landing gently next to Taurik.

They continued in silence until a general rode up to
her side.

The general nodded and said, "I am Boron. Leader of
the Kilian, general of arms for the White City and for you."
He stiffly bowed as one warrior would bow to another.

Sarah was honored by the respect and returned it.

Boron had earned his place beside the lords of the land,
one battle at a time, over the course of many years. His
suntanned body wore the scars of battle. The lines on his
face told of long days squinting into the sun and many

nights in the cold. His leather armor, which clung tightly to his chest, was decorated with symbols of honor. His scarred arms were strong. "May I offer to you a word of caution?" Boron asked.

Sarah was open to any and all suggestions from people who actually knew what they were doing. "Of course," she said without taking her eyes off the path.

"The Dark City is still far off, and our bands grow weary. Should we push through, we will not see victory."

Sarah thought of Tarra. Sarah could feel her. She was scared, alone. Everything in Sarah's being wanted to charge straight through and get Tarra out of there, but she knew Boron was right. They could not save Tarra without a ready army. "Find camp for the night," Sarah said.

Boron nodded and returned to his band.

Within minutes, a scout crew ran past them to find suitable grounds.

With a comforting smile, Taurik said, "Wise choice, Sarah."

Just before nightfall, they reached the camp. The scouts had created a number of small structures for the generals and for Sarah. They also created a fire in the shallow valley.

Boron found Sarah and Taurik and said, "Your rest will be found there." He pointed toward two makeshift structures. "I hope it is to your liking."

"It will be fine. Thank you." Sarah said, realizing how absolutely correct he was to suggest resting.

As Sarah approached her hut, she noticed that Taurik had not left her side. She stopped at the entrance and looked up at him. She was about to say good night but got caught in his eyes and found herself speechless.

Taurik smiled and let her off the hook. "Will I see you for food?"

Sarah caught her breath and replied, "Yes. I believe you will."

With a small bow, Taurik walked over to his hut, leaving Sarah to her thoughts.

The huts were made of woven branches and vines, and a lush fur rug spanned almost the entire width. There were a few blankets made of yarn. Sarah knew the people of Gropal had made them. She relaxed on the comfortable fur, closed her eyes, and let her mind go. Her thoughts started with Tarra. She convinced herself that she would get to her tomorrow—even if it meant her own death. Her mind wandered to Taurik's eyes, his hair, and—with some imagination—his touch.

The smell of cooking meat interrupted her thoughts. She went to the fire, which was twenty feet from her door. The fire was low and wide, and some poor creature was cooking on a spike. Sarah nodded to everyone. She was getting accustomed to the idea that they all knew her. In time, she was certain she would come to know them as well.

Sarah scanned the faces and stopped when she came to Taurik. He smiled and gestured for her to join him. She did so without hesitation.

As they shared their meal, Taurik's company warmed her. He did not say much, but when he did talk, it was purposeful and touching. The meal went too fast for her. She wanted her time with Taurik to continue. Before she knew it, it was time to rest. Rest was not what she wanted, although it was what she needed.

When she stood to leave, Sarah softly took Taurik's hand and led him to her hut. Inside, she turned to him.

"Is everything all right, Sarah?"

Sarah moved to him without breaking eye contact until she was close enough to put her head on his chest. Within moments, she felt his arms encircling her body and pulling her closer. She looked up at him. Before she could say anything, Taurik's lips came down to hers, and it was a long, passionate while before they parted.

His arms grabbed her harder, and he pulled her closer. Taurik pulled back gently, and as their foreheads rested together, he said, "We need to rest."

Sarah knew he was right. Against every physical desire she had, she nodded.

Taurik smiled gently, caressed her face, and left.

When Sarah was alone, she let the softness engulf her aching muscles. By the following night, she would either have Tarra in hand—or she would be dead. That thought made it difficult to get some rest.

As she started to fall asleep, she heard a sound. At first, she couldn't make out what it was, but within moments, she identified it as the sound of marching. Listening for another moment confirmed her suspicion. She shot up and ran out of her hut.

Taurik was standing with Sar and the other generals.

"They found us?" Sarah was ready to gather up her own forces to combat the unseen enemy.

Sar put his hand on Sarah's shoulder and pointed to the far corner of the valley below. "No. Look."

Out from the line of trees, Sarah saw rows of footmen. They wore white-and-red armor, and King Rika was leading them. Behind the king, Sarah could barely make out Sandanti and Grattiella on horseback. War machines of all sizes and thousands of horses with all matter of weaponry crunched through the brush.

The soldiers quickly pitched their tents.

Sarah, Taurik, Sar, and Tinbe went to meet the three as they arrived. A handful of soldiers helped them dismount, tied their steeds, and built them shelters.

Grattiella went to Sarah, and they embraced.

Sandanti smiled and nodded to the generals.

The king put his robed arm around Sarah, and everyone bowed. "Walk with me," he said in a low voice. They walked to a small area in the woods.

"What is it?" Sarah asked.

"It is clear that you have found much strength since you arrived here. Seemingly, you understand that you hold much power. Don't you?" He stopped and looked up at her with a small smile.

Sarah stood in silence, realizing she did not truly know how to answer. She shifted in place.

Rika said, "Ah, Sarah. I didn't think so." He motioned for her to join him at the edge of a small opening in the trees.

As she stood next to him and saw what he was looking at, she had nothing to say. She just looked with honored astonishment at vast army that had been gathering.

"All of them are here for one reason: to protect their queen." Rika unbuckled the robe that draped on his shoulders and turned to Sarah. He swung the garment around her shoulders and fastened it. "Your family has a long history of taking care of the people of this land. I stepped into the seat of king when some of those who were ungrateful turned against your family, murdered your father, and threatened the bloodline of the throne. Your mother was queen, but she decided to leave with you and keep you safe in hopes that you would return when you were ready to accept your position and restore the rightful bloodline. Your father was a great man, a true leader, and my friend. I vowed to them both that I would protect the throne. I have now fulfilled my vow."

"What about my mother? Shouldn't she take the crown?" Sarah was afraid of accepting the responsibility.

"I have spoken to Grattiella. You have come of age and are the chosen one to lead our land back into peace. It has been foretold that you would take the throne of Eslinar." He finished tying the garment and stepped away.

Sarah said, "But I have only started to figure out what my powers are, and I have no idea yet what they mean. How could I possible take the throne?"

"As we all do, Sarah, you will learn. You will see, you will judge, and you will make decisions that affect many." He put his arm around her again, and they began walking back to the huts. "You will make many mistakes."

Sarah looked to him.

He smiled and continued, "As we all do. Your heart is pure, and no decision comes from the dark place. You will do justice to and for your people."

"Do I have a choice?" she asked as they came to the dwindling fire. She looked around at her smiling generals. They were silently awaiting an answer.

Sarah turned to Grattiella, Sandanti, and the generals. "Seems I have some thinking to do." She went back to her hut.

When Taurik stood to go with her, Tinbe grabbed his arm and said, "Her decision to make, it is." He let go his grip.

Taurik sat back down and looked at Sarah's hut.

In her hut, Sarah paced back and forth, taking care not to trip on the rug. "You're kidding me! What if I don't want to? What if I can't do it?" She stopped pacing and pictured many moments with her mother. She sat down and realized that every moment, every lesson, and every argument with her mother had led her to where she was. She had been groomed from birth to believe in herself, to take pride in what she did, and to be conscientious of others. It was the people around her who made her doubt herself and her abilities. Her mother always taught her that she was meant for greatness and would do great things in life. Sarah bowed her head and took a deep breath.

The flap that covered the entrance to the hut opened, and Grattiella walked in. Grattiella sat next to Sarah and put her arm around her.

"All my life, I thought you were being metaphoric," Sarah said.

Grattiella said, "You have taken in all of this with the strength I have always known you had. It is a big deal. You have been presented with an entirely new existence. The question you need to answer for yourself is if you accept it."

Sarah looked at her mom like a child and asked, "Do I have a choice?"

Grattiella smiled, stood, and walked to the door. "You always have a choice, Sarah. You always have."

Sarah saw that Grattiella had dropped something. She picked up what turned out to be an amulet. Sarah's surroundings started to fade, and the room was replaced with scene after scene of time and space. She saw her birth, the face of her father, and her mother shielding her from harm during an attack on the White City. She saw the tears shed when her mother made the choice to leave her home and her known existence to save her daughter (the heir to the kingdom) and the sadness in the faces of the ones Grattiella was leaving behind. Sarah saw countless warriors, dirt, swords, cannons, and blood. She saw scared villagers huddling for safety and clips of every battle that had gone on before. It was very much like the battle she had seen of Sar's family. Finally, she saw the ongoing magic battle and its impact upon the lands.

Sarah let go of the medallion, and it dropped to the ground with a thud. She quickly put her hand out to the nearest support beam to catch herself and her spinning head. She found a fur blanket in the corner and pulled it over her head for warmth. As slumber came to her weary eyes, Sarah knew just what she had to do.

Before dreams could take hold, a stocky woman walked in.

Sarah's eyes began to focus, and she realized it was Vente. Sarah sat up, smiled, and said, "It's good to see you."

Vente replied, "As well to you, Miss Sarah."

Vente prepared the small pile of cloth and adornments she had entered with. With one item in her hand, Vente helped Sarah to her feet. With a gleam in her eyes, Vente motioned for Sarah to bend forward a hair and lifted a crown onto her head.

Sarah saw it as it passed her eyes. It was a finely woven band of darkened wood intertwined with the most beautiful metal she had ever seen. It looked delicate, but it felt sturdy. It fit perfectly under her loosely tasseled hair.

Vente took a few strands of hair from each section, and before Sarah knew it, the beautiful ornament was as much a part of her head as her hair was.

Within minutes, Sarah didn't even feel it anymore. It went from being a burden to being a reason to stand taller than ever.

Once Vente was satisfied with Sarah's headpiece, she reached for the cape that was to be worn by the queen and proudly draped the beautiful tapestry over Sarah's shoulders.

Sarah took a minute alone to breathe deeply before walking out of her hut. When she approached, the generals stood.

Sar nodded and smiled proudly. Tinbe, Boron, and the others did the same.

Sarah saw Taurik by the ridge, overlooking the valley. Spirit was at his side.

Grattiella and Sandanti stepped out from a hut.

Sarah walked to Taurik and touched his shoulder. She went to her mother and placed the medallion in her hand.

Grattiella nodded.

Sarah replaced Taurik at Spirit's side and walked Spirit to the ridge.

Within moments, all the warriors were silent and looking up at her. Sarah unbelted the cape from around her neck and draped the cloth over the back of Spirit. She said, "Over the course of my life, I have learned a lot of things, but never as much as I have since I arrived here in my homeland. It has been through your strength that I have seen truth—and through your strength that I have learned truth. It has been with your blood that my homeland *is*—and I will not stand by for one moment as witness to stolen innocence. I will not stand by idly while loved ones are tortured and their spirits are darkened to life's beauty. You have proven your strength, courage, and honor time and again. I stand here before you now, knowing that I have been chosen. I also stand before you to remind you that all of you have a choice. If you choose not to follow me, you may leave untarnished and with no guilt. If you should choose to follow me, then I will follow you—and in *your* strength, I will lead!"

The warriors raised their staffs, spears, and shields, released their battle cries, struck their weapons on the ground three times, and dropped to their knees. With heads bowed, they stayed there for many moments.

When they stood, Sarah nodded, directed the troops to gather their effects, and went back to her generals.

"Well done," Boron said to Sarah as she entered their circle.

Sarah said, "Diversion is the only way we will all get what we are setting out for today. I need one team to attack the front gate to the city. Inside those gates, there are shops and homes. There will be many to fight, but when I was there, there were many who were not there of their own free will. They are innocent in this fight—unless they make it their own. Make it known to your men to leave them unharmed. If we have what we set out for today, they will rebuild when all is done. The other team needs to go to the southwest gate. The same rules apply. If we can separate their forces within the city, we stand some chance of defeating them."

"Divide and conquer," Grattiella said with a smile.

"That's the idea." Sarah returned the grin.

"And you?" Taurik asked.

"I will go to the north wing with Spirit. Tarra is still there. I saw her. She is strong but tiring quickly. Today we bring her home."

Sarah got on Spirit's back, and they rode into the forest. Once they hit a clearing, they took flight with ease and doubled back, keeping a steady pattern just above the trees and behind the army. The attempt she was about to make depended on her army getting there first.

Soon, the White Army of Eslinar was on the move. Quickly and quietly, they moved through the forest.

Sarah watched through the treetops. The closer they got to their target, the better she felt. She held hope for the innocent in the Dark City, hope for the safety of those in Eslinar, and hope for Tarra.

Sarah closed her eyes and tried to see her. The connection between them was strong. She reached out to Tarra and told her to hold on.

⊠ Chapter 15

WITHIN AN HOUR, THEY REACHED THE BORDER TO THE DARK City. Under the cover of the trees, Sarah saw Boron and Taurik parade before the men. She could not make out what they said, but after a momentary pause, a battle cry rose over the land.

Her army charged, but before they reached the main gate, thousands of soldiers ran out. A steady stream of arrows began to fly over the wall.

The Dark Army had been warned. Sarah saw the others wrap around to flank the city at the eastern gate as planned. They were met with dark warriors and arrows. Men from both sides began to fall.

Sarah could see a narrow area that wasn't in chaos. To her delight, it was right where she had hoped—even though it was a bit smaller than she had anticipated.

As Sarah and Spirit approached the north tower, there was no place for Spirit to land. She directed Spirit to get as close as possible to the top of the tower. When they got there, Spirit hovered for a moment as Sarah gently dismounted. She perched on a tiny ledge and looked at

Spirit. When their eyes met, Sarah gave a grateful smile and patted Spirit's neck.

Sarah watched Spirit fly out of sight and hoped the horse would be safe. She looked around for a way to get inside the tower. She shuffled along the perimeter, holding her body tightly against the wall.

When Sarah made her way around, she looked down on the battle at the front gate. Men, women, and beasts were entrenched in battle. Sounds were not clear from her vantage point, but she could see swords on swords, hand-to-hand combat, and the thumping of a battering ram. Sarah saw something she did not expect to see. There was a commotion inside the city walls. A fire burned. The city was also doing battle from the inside.

Sarah was filled with the breath of possible victory, which she had not felt until that moment.

Her focus returned to the precarious nature of her footing as she made her way over to a small set of cobblestone stairs. They were as narrow as her small feet, but she made her way over to an upper window.

Sarah looked around to make sure no one was there. Seeing that it was an unoccupied circular room, she climbed in. Taking great care to be quiet, she made her way to the doorway of the tiny room. Before exiting, she took a minute to listen. The sounds she heard were distant. She stuck her head out through the arched doorway, but there were no exits or entrances on either side. She would have to get to the end of the hall quickly since there was nowhere to duck if anyone saw her.

As Sarah reached the end of the hallway, five soldiers ran past in clanking armor. Sarah hit her head on the wall when she slammed back into it in a desperate attempt to evade detection. The soldiers were more focused on getting where they were going than on their current surroundings.

Sarah knew Tarra was in the north tower. She could feel her, but she did not know exactly where. She ducked into a small room to think. She closed her eyes and said, "Where are you?"

Letting her mind's eye take control, she saw that Tarra was locked in a cage and more weary than she had ever been. Sarah knew there was only a short time before she would lose Tarra altogether. The Dark Lord's power engulfed the spirit one piece at a time. Tarra had fought it off, but she was growing tired. She would eventually give in to the darkness—or she would die.

As Sarah searched her vision for landmarks, doors, or windows, she felt electricity roll over her skin. It was a new sensation. It didn't hurt. Was it a new power? She focused more on the vision, but she only saw one door. If she went in, she would be trapped.

Down.

Sarah took off with her sword drawn. It felt comfortable in her hand. Sarah was ready for combat, and with every corner turned, she could feel Tarra more.

Sarah stopped at the entrance to a narrow hallway. A burning lantern hung in one corner. She peered around the corner to see if anyone was there. To her horror, she saw a huge, snarling, horned beast covered in slime.

Sarah stepped back. *You're kidding, right?*

She only had her sword, the goblet, the pot, and the medallion. She was thankful she had grabbed them when she left the White Castle, but she had a feeling they were not meant for that kind of fight.

She unwrapped the small pot and threw it to the other side of the hall. With her sword ready, she waited as the beast ran to see what the noise was.

Sarah heard it get closer, and with a deep breath, she ran to cross the beast's path. With a tremendous thrust, she used the beast's momentum combined with some of her own to slash through its throat. When it landed, its head was held on only by fibers of flesh.

Sarah could not stop her momentum and slammed into the far wall, which dazed her for a moment. The beast on the floor was bleeding a thick, mucus-like blood. Sarah felt the electricity in her veins again and realized the sensation was linked to her sudden astounding strength. Sarah was momentarily leery of her new strength. She did not know how to control it, and it was not the best time to begin learning, but it did feel good to singlehandedly take down a beast of that size.

Sarah grabbed the keys the beast had been protecting and opened the door. After taking care to leave it open, she took the keys to be safe.

It was dark, but as her eyes adjusted, she could make out a cavern filled with boulders. She followed another narrow walkway down through an opening between two large rocks. Walking slowly past them, in case they were booby trapped, the room opened up into a large space of dirt and stone.

Small fires burned along the walls, but they gave little light and even less warmth. On the far end, Sarah saw the cage from her visions. She ran to it and wrapped her hands around the bars. "Tarra! Tarra! Are you okay?"

There was barely any movement, but Tarra whispered, "Yes. Please hurry."

Sarah pulled and tugged, but it was futile. She examined the bars on the cage. Walking around the perimeter, she looked for any sign of weakness. *The lock!*

Sarah remembered very little from her schooling, but she did remember that electricity would get hot if channeled correctly. She wondered for a moment if her skin would be able to withstand the heat, but she decided to find out.

Sarah wrapped her hands around the lock, shut her eyes, and focused as hard as she could. She could feel the warmth building between her palms, and the metal began heating up. She focused hard, and the metal began to smoke. She knew it was taking too long.

Just as she was about to give up, she felt a small hand placed on her own. Tarra had joined her. They focused together, and in a very short time, the lock turned red.

Sarah bent it easily until it broke in two, opened the door, and scooped up Tarra.

Tarra did not look well; her skin was pale, and she looked like she had not been fed in days.

"I couldn't get out by myself," Tarra said softly.

Sarah caressed Tarra's hair and replied, "And I couldn't get in by myself. Drink this." Sarah poured some of the water from her canteen into Tarra's mouth and hung the medallion around Tarra's neck for as much protection as it would allow. "We will move soon. First, get a little water into you."

Sarah sat back to catch her breath and was hit from behind by a single blow of light. She landed with a thud at the base of the far wall. She rolled over and tried to get the air back into her lungs. She looked up and saw Arron walking toward Tarra.

"Get away for her!" Sarah ran to get between them.

"You should have stayed with me, dear Sarah, but I will be satisfied with this one in your place." He smiled menacingly.

Sarah was filled with dread. When Tarra tried to move, Sarah's fear was replaced by rage. Her skin began to feel electric again, and before she knew what she was doing, she sent a jet of electricity straight at Arron. It knocked him across the room.

"You have found your powers, my dear Sarah." Arron chuckled, stood up, and brushed the dirt from his clothes.

"I am not your dear, and I have found my powers—no thanks to you!" Sarah tried desperately to keep it from him that she had just found out about that last one.

"I could have tutored you in how to wield them. Your powers could have been very strong." Arron slowly moved toward Tarra.

Sarah gathered her inner strength and said, "How do you know they're not?" Without warning, she struck him with another blast. It hit a wall, and the rocks crumbled on top of Arron.

He chuckled again and got up from underneath them. "Now that is interesting." He was smiling.

She sent a blast of heat toward his legs. His knees buckled, and he was thrown back against the wall, dizzying him for a moment.

Tarra sat up and no longer looked pained.

Sarah felt a large amount of relief. She knew she could not defeat Arron alone, but they stood a chance together.

Before the Dark Lord could regain his footing, Sarah hit him square in the chest, throwing him back hard. When her electric beam hit the wall, it opened a small hole, and the sunlight came through.

It was clear to Sarah that Arron did not want her to be with Tarra. She could tell he knew he stood no chance against their combined powers.

Tarra stood and looked at Arron. He was bleeding, and there was fear in his eyes.

Sarah knew she had to act right away. She took a step toward Tarra, but she was thrown against the wall again.

The Dark Lord held her there for a few seconds and walked closer to Tarra.

Tarra began to back away, and Sarah yelled, "Don't let him touch you, Tarra!"

With that, the grip on her got stronger. She was suffocating. Sarah could feel her heartbeat in her neck, and the blood was starting to slow in her veins. She could not let that be the end of it. She had learned too much and come too far to give up. She had to get out from the Dark Lord's grip.

Sarah noticed that Arron was having a hard time keeping his grip on her and focusing on catching Tarra. She finally saw her chance.

Each time the Dark Lord lunged for Tarra, his grip lightened on Sarah. It might be enough if she rested for a moment. She knew it would be dangerous because her body might give in to the pain and lack of oxygen, but she had to try. Sarah let her body go limp, and she hit the floor.

The Dark Lord began to chuckle. It became louder as he walked closer to Sarah's body. "Did you really think you could come into my world and defeat me?" He turned from Sarah and started walking back to Tarra.

Tarra was crying as she looked back and forth between Sarah and the Dark Lord.

"Did you, little one, think she would save you? You will be mine—and so will your power."

Tarra stopped crying and stood tall.

The Dark Lord closed in on Tarra and said, "There is only one way out of this dark place for you—and it is through me!"

Sarah decided he would have to be taken care of the old-fashioned way. She quietly positioned herself behind him and yelled, "There is always another way out!" She punched him in the face as hard as she could and knocked him clean on his tail. She grabbed Tarra's hand, and they sent a blast toward the wall with the tiny sunlit hole.

Within a second, the room was filled with daylight—and Arron was buried under a ton of boulders and rubble.

Sarah and Tarra climbed out onto a very small ledge. If it collapsed, they would splinter on the rocks below. If they missed the rocks, the impact with the water in the moat would snap their necks.

Under their feet, they felt rumbling from inside the wall. It grew louder and more violent.

Sarah could feel the part of the wall they were leaning on getting weaker.

Rocks tumbled past them, and Tarra began to cry.

Sarah looked around for a way off the ledge or something to hold. There was nothing. The rumbling got louder, and the falling rocks became more massive and frequent.

Sarah saw something on the wind: two horses and one rider. Within seconds, they were in front of Sarah.

"Give me the child!" Boron yelled.

Sarah looked at Tarra and lifted her up.

Boron grabbed her, put her in front of him, and flew away.

Sarah pivoted her weight to jump onto Spirit's back, but the stones beneath Sarah's feet gave way. She fell, but Spirit quickly darted down and caught her. She landed on Spirit's back, and they pulled up a few feet above the ground.

As they flew away, Sarah looked back once. The tower crumbled down on Arron, eliminating any further threats from his darkness.

As they got farther from the battle, it grew quieter. She rested her head on Spirit's mane and stayed there for a long time as they flew over the waters, forests, and valleys.

When they neared Eslinar, Spirit lifted her head a little to alert Sarah that it was time to straighten up. Although she could still feel the warm blood dripping down her leg and the sting of the air grazing the wounds on her arms, she sat as straight as she could.

Spirit circled the tower of the White Castle and landed without a hitch on the top of its highest peak. Sarah dismounted Spirit with a slide, and as she tried to walk away, she lost her balance. Spirit was there again to hold her up. Sarah rested her head on Spirit's brow and rubbed Spirit's neck. They stood together until Sarah heard footsteps coming from the doorway at the edge of the rooftop.

"Sarah!" Grattiella ran toward her daughter.

Sarah took her mother's arm and let herself be examined. "Where is Tarra?"

"Inside. She will heal in time. Come on. We should tend to you right now."

Sarah was far too tired and physically pained to argue. She allowed her mother to lead her down from the tower.

After passing through many gorgeous hallways, Grattiella helped Sarah undress in her living quarters.

Sarah took a warm bath and washed off the fear, darkness, and blood from the fight.

Loosely wrapped in fine linens, Sandanti entered and began nursing Sarah's wounds. As soon as she put the ointment on the wounds, they began to heal. Sandanti called for food, and servants set food on a small table near the bed.

"Please eat," Grattiella said.

Sarah nodded and began to nibble, but she had no appetite. All she could think of was Tarra. She needed to see her, and she needed to see her right then. Sarah stood up and went to the wardrobe.

Sandanti stood at attention and said, "What in the name—"

"If I am well enough to eat, I am well enough to go to her." Sarah found a loose-fitting sleeveless gown in the wardrobe and slipped it on over her wounds. She put on a pair of leather slippers and stood at the door, realizing she didn't know where Tarra was resting. "Please, Mother?" she said softly.

Grattiella put down the linens, approached Sarah, and kissed her on her forehead. "Follow me, you stubborn girl."

A few hallways later, they entered Tarra's room. She

was sitting up in her bed, and Tinbe was reading to her. Sarah smiled.

Sar and Boron were also there. They had stayed to keep watch over Tarra while Sarah was being tended to. They both nodded to Sarah as she entered, and Sarah returned the gesture. She came to the bed and sat.

Tinbe had stopped reading when Sarah entered.

"Please go on," Sarah said.

They all sat and enjoyed the end of the fairy tale.

When the story was done, Tinbe closed the book and put it back in his satchel. He grinned and looked at Tarra and Sarah and then back at Tarra. "Care for her, you will take. Right?"

Tarra giggled and smiled. "Yes, I will."

Sarah was giggling as much as her two broken ribs would allow.

Sarah heard a shuffling at the door, and when she looked, Grattiella was speaking with Taurik. He had bloodstained bandages on his head, and a sling held his left arm in place. He looked over toward Sarah, and his face lightened.

Boron walked to the bed and put his hand on Sarah's head. "It was a good fight, Sarah," he said as he walked her to the door. "Now you need to heal from it."

Sarah kept walking, but she looked back at Tarra. Sandanti was brushing her hair.

"She will be fine," Boron said. "Go."

Sarah took Grattiella's arm, and they walked back to Sarah's suite with Taurik.

In her room, the draperies had been pulled back. A sea of light poured in, and Sarah noticed what a beautiful place it was. She sat at the small table opposite her bed and smiled at her mother. "I'll be okay."

"I never doubted it." Grattiella kissed Sarah's forehead, nodded to Taurik, and took her leave.

Taurik joined Sarah at the table.

Sarah said, "I'm sorry you were hurt."

Taurik chuckled and replied, "Not nearly as hurt as I would have been."

Sarah looked puzzled.

"Apparently you made quite an impression during your short stay in the Dark City," Taurik said.

"How's that? I hardly spoke to anyone."

Adjusting his sling, Taurik said, "They, as we did, knew who you were, and your presence alone brought hope. The hope in the few who saw you there was enough to inspire others who were loyal to the goodness that city once held. They were ready to do their parts when the time came."

"The fire inside the city walls?" Sarah asked.

"Yes. Had it not been for them, we would not have been able to take the day. Since they weakened the city's defenses from within while we were attacking both sides, our men had a chance. And it was a good one, as it turns out."

"How many were lost?" Sarah asked quietly, afraid of the answer.

Taurik took her hand in his good one. "We lost many, but those of us who fought with you did so willingly. You are good, and your cause was a good one. In the end, the ones who died, live on through the freedom regained by the people who live there."

"Still." Sarah shook her head, knowing her decision had cost them their lives.

Taurik took Sarah's hand and said, "You made your decision to lead them—to help protect the futures of Tarra and all of us. You gave them the option to join you in your fight or depart without guilt. You handled yourself as a queen, as a woman of compassion and dignity." He kissed her hand, stood up, and gently pulled her up with him. "I am proud just to know you." He took her chin in his hand and kissed her gently on the lips.

Sarah returned Taurik's kiss willingly. His lips were warm, and his intentions were pure. When their lips parted, they lingered for a moment.

Sarah bowed her head and rested it upon Taurik's chest. For a few minutes, she listened to his heart and felt the warmth of his body. She gazed into his beautiful eyes, sat back down, and said, "Thank you."

"For what?" Taurik stroked Sarah's hair away from her face.

"For everything." Sarah went to the window to look out over the lands. "You helped guide me from the beginning, and when I fell, you were there to catch me. You helped me when I needed it most. Thank you."

"I certainly didn't do that on my own." Taurik chuckled as he joined Sarah at the window. Taking her hand, he kissed it and looked at her again.

"You need your rest." He looked down at his arm and added, "As do I. There is still much that needs to be done. I will call on you later perhaps?"

"I would very much like that," Sarah said.

After another gentle but passionate kiss, Taurik left.

Sarah was alone. The breeze passed over her skin, and she closed her eyes to enjoy the sensation. She took a deep breath, and as she exhaled, she remembered sitting on the hotel balcony at the start of her vacation. It seemed like a million years earlier. Then she remembered her bag.

She opened her eyes and saw her pack in the corner. She reached in and let out a sigh of relief. She pulled out her journal and sat down at the table.

For a moment, she examined the tattered cover. Some spots had been wet and dried again. Other areas had tears. She thought that it had held up really well given what it had gone through.

Opening the pages, she began to read some of her entries. When she was done, Sarah sat back and reflected on all that had taken place since the start of her journey. She stared at the blank page next to her last entry. She picked up her small pencil and began to write:

The End of a New Day

I have been through and learned too much to log. One lesson that should not go unmentioned is that I spent far too much time comparing my old life with this new one. I have come to see that there is no old life or new life. There is just *my* life. My journey, so far, it certainly is an awesome one.

I have grown stronger in so many ways since this adventure began. I grow stronger still and have been placed among wonderful folks who can help guide me in learning how to use my powers. I do look forward to that.

Nothing could have prepared me for my true purpose—or the experiences themselves. The hard things, scary things, and even some of the trivial things are to be marveled at. They taught me so much. I have been asked if I will stay, and for now, my answer is most definitely yes.